W9-BSQ-736

I wish to share with the reader a few years of my life, mostly around the time when it was immortal. To be more specific, it will encompass the years from 1928 to 1932. I will be as objective as I can, but as it is I am human and it is no secret that this is impossible.

Also, I must add that I am not here to woo the reader with different thought other than his own. At the very least I hope to render validation and confirmation of its existing condition, and, with any luck, enrich its purpose further by my prosaic experience.

And yet, on another parallel, we hear and see things from the same angle that confirm and encourage our current behavior. The following may indirectly pivot, however slightly and almost innocently, this profile of thought.

In some other words, the following is nothing new.

This book, as with anything decent or anything involving goodness I have attempted in my life, is dedicated to Mary.

-Paul McNamara October 7, 1998

PROLOGUE

Complicating a moment is the first instinct of man. Worrying about that moment is his close second. It is not until several layers have been peeled back do we get to real purpose, if ever. Indeed, the senses are the unsung heroes of existence but always seem to be trumped and trampled by the tormented tempest in the mind. Our physical attributes may make most men clever at manipulating the world, yet *consciousness* makes us fools every one. Although deny it we do, it is against human nature to be wise.

Luckily for us there's a confidence in ignorance that true wisdom can never obtain, even in dreams. With that in mind, I sing to myself,

However the moment is purchased within,
Past eternity, the timeline is thin.
Spend a lifetime setting truth a liar,
Deceived by hope and sophistry and desire.

Through self-preservation and insolence, our thoughts are suspiciously lined with immortality. Our habits in most ways prove similar, as if things in life continue uninterrupted; as if we had a greater lifespan of a star and were to live forever. A wonderful trait, no doubt, but at the end of the day it is as equally self-destructive. We keep a blind eye to the reality of it, relying on subcategories and the tried and almost true efforts like tradition and repetition. In this current society we most often miss the mark, becoming prisoners to our own beliefs; with inflated and overestimated quotes of self-worth; ostentatious appraisals of importance in an overstocked and flooded market; values bought that cannot be afforded; where a pound is not worth a penny, and with taxes, of course, not included. Therefore and quite naturally, the world is wrought with unsatisfied customers at pandemic proportions.

Yet often do we arm ourselves with coping skills of insipid labors and hobbies to pass time, in turn directly wasting it; flat-lining or even digressing the self instead of improving it; staring at the clock like it was some lost lover, until it finally stops ticking and falls off the wall. It is an old and tired fate some have written about and know very well, most others not at all, and, for whatever reason, remains for the most part un-evolved, untaught, and unimagined. Like the stars we cannot see in the night sky, the weaknesses in our nature are difficult to count, and in spite of all the wonderful concentrations of thought throughout history, we continue to make no advances or improvements in any of them. And so we not only miss the mark in life, we also miss the point.

At the same time though and at some level, most of us seem quite satisfied to remain at the superficial crust of ourselves. We delight in simple pleasures and simple sorrows; crying rivers of joy or sadness that often hardly deserve a tear. We never scrape past our dermis, never sweep away more than dust. It's that which we dare not dig deeper; and would rather spend a lifetime to manicure our lawn than nourish the soil; prefer a pretty flower than a *root ne plus ultra*. There indeed is some truth in our reluctance, for our hesitation dwells on the fears of what we may find. But nonetheless, life is shallow enough.

My friend Plato, as he was aptly nicknamed, said to me once, "Deserve your life. Never stop earning the potential of it." So much easier said, I suppose, than done, but by no means less important or demanding less effort by default. It is hard to deserve something so precious and fleeting, yet somehow we find it easier to forget that it is. Slowly and submissively do we become bewitched by living; conditioned to a numbness not yet entirely labeled or defined but immediately identified. We want life easier, happier; we work hard for it, smooth out the bumps, and then find it tedious and dull. The moment our dreams of safety and security are obtained we long for the days when we had nothing, when the thoughts of risk and uncertainty consumed us. 'Tis the human condition running on all cylinders with no known vaccine or cure, only because there can't be one, for it would directly and completely contradict what it is to be labeled as such.

But no matter the threat or circumstance, meaning continues to survive. There remains that blinding force; that numbing of all reasoning; the deadening of all common sense; the most offensive annoyance to reality; the wonderful and most powerful thing in creation: *hope*. Our will to live and see the sun rise tomorrow is unrivaled. A brighter, better day to come, so we *hope*, not realizing the day we are in can be the best and brightest we have ever seen. As the imperturbable Thoreau once wrote, "There is no value in life except what you choose to place upon it and no happiness in any place except what you bring to it yourself."

Perspective *is* everything. I almost would say perspective is almost everything, but it's not. Perspective is *everything*. Just as I have found that the people who have money worry about that money more than the people who don't have money worry about the money they don't have. Thoreau, with his quiet observation and seemingly gifted ability to tackle the monkey-wrenches of life, went on to write, "I know of no more encouraging fact than the unquestionable ability of man to elevate his life by a conscious endeavour."

As out of favor as it is, I have blind devotion to this. Most people I know consistently and unconsciously complain of their position in life as if they were bullied into a corner, physically threatened or mentally tortured in some sort of constrained and claustrophobic quicksand. An old friend of mine believed that he had bad luck since the day he was born. He complained of his work, his wife, his family, his finance, his life. He talked like he was treading water in a bottomless pit of stress, with his nose and mouth barely breaking the surface to take air. He could not comprehend the notion that man makes the majority of his own luck as much as he makes the majority of his own anxiety. He would want to step outside and try to fist fight me if I told him that *he* was insulting his own intelligence. Of course my friend never found any other choice but to visit his well stocked liquor cabinet early and often, not only to quench his thirst, but to help make the world more bearable on his shoulders when in truth the world suffered from the weight of him.

I know of parents who act in similar fashion when it comes to their children. They of course would never trade their offspring for the world, but if given the chance to do it all over again, would have second thoughts in reproduction. Since now in possession of them, and, taking for granted like most of us do with the wonderful things in life, they talk as if they were forced to reproduce, as if they were held at gunpoint to conceive. To be sure, in this subject as in others, most never understand that it is they who are holding the gun to their own heads themselves.

People often keep reminding me that life was not meant to be enjoyed. I keep forgetting. They keep reminding me. They seem to be unhappy because they remember happier times; or they are unhappy because they remember unhappy times; or they see others happier than they see themselves; or more unhappy; and at the end of the day, whether they realize it or admit it or not, for whatever reason, no matter how they get there, they usually end up being unhappy. Far worse are those who fake themselves as being happy and tell others all too often how much they are, when their private behavior and quiet moments alone prove otherwise. Lives are often crippled by the very things we are told and led to believe bring happiness. The miseries in life that most of us suffer are not innate, but learned.

And so the deception is favored as the ideals of life become murky. To obtain one is to no longer need one and sometimes, as the saying goes, not much is worse than getting what one wished for. In this present and strained society, we strut around thinking we are free and can do whatever we want, when all we want is to do what everyone else is doing. We forget that free will remains an illusion and long extinct is the idea of an original thought. Certainly nothing is new from me. Not one thing. I recycle thoughts from others. I have leaned on the shoulders of great philosophers. I steal from their minds to enrich my own. I plagiarize my parents. I take from my mother. I plunder my father. I've pillaged them my entire life. And yet equally am I restrained by them too.

We seem to run parallel with our lives; never are we in them. They are just out of reach. It is only after some time do we stop for a moment, remember, look over, and become lost or confused because they are unfamiliar and cannot be recognized. They are either too far ahead or behind, or we are; at each moment jockeying for position; finding the finish line a wall where we can do nothing but look back. It never dawns on most of us to ever look over or, for that matter, anywhere at all.

So channeled are we from the start, born into that over trodden, standardized downhill groove of education and belief, that worn out and stagnant machine of society; our chances of anything original are nil. We dream about things that already are, not of things that are not; mindlessly focusing toward all things that are within the conditioned bubble. We dare not burst that bubble to see beyond or around. Worse yet, we do not know there is a bubble to begin with and let ourselves and our thoughts become desperate and domesticated, turning a deaf ear to the cries of our inner soul that was born to do otherwise. "We were not designed to be fenced in," my friend Plato said to me once, "Man becomes the perpetrator and victim of himself."

I don't pretend to be above or below or outside of this. I've got both feet in it. As I stand here on my soapbox, I am a coward only and almost exclusively to myself. I easily insult my intelligence every day. Sometimes though, I can and *do* step away from it. I'd like to admit that over the years I've become proficient at it; at times almost unconscious to it, creating certain paths that are now well known and well worn on me. For instance, often and almost involuntarily, no matter what I am doing, I can transcend myself some fifty years into the future and look back onto the very moment I am in. Any graded annoyance soon turns to delicate and contented reflection; and when I return to reality and take my bearing, the present moment becomes that much more wonderful. I never pretend to believe I'm the happiest person in the world, but I would argue that I am just as happy as the least sad. True contentment of self is often found in the thoughts one has when one is alone.

But there is no doubt that the exterior always plays some part, no matter how small, on the interior. The problem lies with those who depend entirely on these outside sources. I have never sought meaning in these motives, but it's true that meaning in them often found me. There were times when I have travelled to far off places to find myself, neglecting the orphic intuition that I was never lost to begin with, and would only then discover myself upon returning home.

External love, of course, of any form can be boundless. Mary, my wife of over 60 years opened gates and doors of a kind I never knew I had. For me to care for her like I did and for her to do likewise gave me a purpose beyond meaning. She was my outside source, my *raison d'etres*. Ninety-nine parts of life out of one hundred are repetitive and forgettable. In theory and in practice, man really only lives a few moments, regardless of years. Memories are condensed from a life of 70 years to perhaps 7 days, and even then that week is a stretch to fill. The one part of my life that my memory was consumed with was Mary. I have no doubt that the last thought I have, as was so with my first remembered one, will involve her.

He was only known to most as Plato, but his real name was Jonathan Grant. He was my dearest and most important friend I met while in New York City, and for that matter, throughout my entire life. He instilled a conscious intent in me from the moment I met him. He was my catalyst, my trigger, my ground zero to thought. Despite his core understanding of the state of man and the realities of things, he still believed in it *all.* His teachings were not how to sustain life, but to inspire it. It wasn't that he held class, for he only taught by example, believing in harnessing all the good in life and riding it as long as you can, and re-channeling the bad that occurs as an energy source. Tears, as an example, interested him immensely and although I only saw him cry once, he talked about them often. He was fascinated by the fact that we were the sole creatures that not only did so, but also *needed to.* The night we snuck up to the top of the Empire State Building he said to me, "Tears require an abundance of energy, but their redemption can recreate a power that is one hundred fold." This, coincidentally, was also the same and only time I saw him cry.

One of the last things Plato wrote to me was this: "I swear, if found with very little hope in existence; if, by irrepressible circumstances, life in this world has diminished the ember to live in it; when all else fails, when all other efforts have dead-ended, find a quiet and high spot facing eastward, wake early before a cloud, and witness the rising sun. Stare into that star until your eyelids flutter extemporaneously; and like the light that fills earth and sky, so too will it fill the mind and soul with promise, re-aligning life with what is, to what could be."

The following begins with our meeting and ends a few years thereafter at our departure. Plato would, I think, be almost proud of me. Tears helped write this story.

1

At the time I was eighteen going on infinity. I was straddling two seasons where childhood and manhood often quarreled, where one resisted to let go while the other hesitated to take over; where each took turns cursing, injuring and mending one another; eventually making amends and truce through compromise and covenant as their horizons slowly expanded and contracted accordingly. It was a time where the heart knew for certain it will live forever and the soul aged no more, not for a second, for the rest of its life.

I was not so much full of myself as I was of living, even though the former often gave the latter a run for its money. Every molecule of my being was eating up each moment and looking forward to the next; while fondness of my short collected past gave push to contribute to its history. I was endlessly raw with life and not anywhere close to being burned and bored by experience. What added to my unbounded ambition was that I was in love, most fervently, with someone infinitely more than myself. Mary Fisk and I knew each other from the beginning of time and were determined to be together at the end of it.

"*Hey*," she whispered one late morning as we were sun drying ourselves after a swim on our favorite bank of the Connecticut River, the day before I was to leave her, to move to New York City, to go to college at New York University, to play football there on an athletic scholarship; to go to a place where I knew not one soul and not to see Mary again until Christmas, nearly four months from then, "Why don't we just say the hell with it and get married now?"

Mary's humor was extremely cotton-mouthed, even for someone from New Hampshire. Her brilliance was not in her words but in her delivery. She most always wore a serious face, although every so often she grew a smirk that never really quite curved but rather straightened on each side of her mouth, very similar to the one she wore at this moment. Beautiful though it was, her face carried a preoccupied disposition, as if in the middle of solving a problem or aiming an arrow with a bow. Her short cropped hair complimented her character, with a neck line and set of shoulders that carried a subtle yet distinguished toughness. To a stranger she would have seemed unapproachable, but to me she was just the opposite. In short, she had the heart of a sunrise yet the peaceful and contemplating soul of one setting.

She could have cared less if we were married or not, or anything or not, just as long as we were together. Mary was too clever and tough to fall victim to any tradition, belief, or cultural norm; the fake-ness of society as she called it, the *lies layered.* She said it for no other reason than to tease me for she knew all too well that I fell for a few of them, marriage not excluded.

I only smiled, knowing her too well, knowing she didn't want an answer, because her question didn't mean to have one.

"I'm almost positive I can fit you in my suitcase, Mary," I responded.

The days and nights of that summer before my first year of college stretched out like the salt water taffy we used to make together on Sunday evenings. Time was slipping away, as time had long been famous for, and life as we only knew it was soon to become a fast and fond memory.

"I'm not going to be able to do this," Mary said with an inner voice, almost thinking to herself, as she was drying herself off with a towel from our swim that same day before I was to leave her.

I said nothing but looked at her with the same expression she gave me. We were together for so long, best friends since the first grade, sitting next to each other on our first day of school, scared as much now as we were then.

"It's not a part of me to be no longer a part of you," she sighed.

Her posture gave a little, as if giving up the fight of our departure. Her eyes began to flutter and glisten, as though a cold wind carrying dust and debris had picked up all at once. She reached down into her little bag she brought with her everywhere she went. It had a perfectly embroidered chickadee on a bottom corner. Her grandmother made it for her for Christmas one year and Mary cherished it more than anything.

She pulled out a necklace from it and handed it to me.

"Here," she whispered.

I took it from her hands and examined it closely. The material was something familiar, tightly woven into a braid that was light brown in color, perhaps the thickness of a pencil, ending with a clasp on one end and a hook on the other.

"Mary," I whispered back, all at once realizing its source, "This, is your hair!"

Four years before, as we were entering high school, Mary and her parents quarreled about her curfew and her slack in devotion to the family business. Her father was a butcher and every meal or snack in her entire life up to that point involved some sort of carnivorous concoction. She was sick of it: sick of cutting it, sick of preparing it, and she was sick of eating it. And as her parents knew all too well, she had a hard time being told what to do.

In defiance she cut off all of the beautiful hair that reached past her waist, and went from a pretty little girl to a homely looking little boy. In some ways I was glad of it, for I knew how beautiful she was both on the outside and in, but mostly because the other boys in town stopped hitting on her. Well, at least for a while.

I never thought I'd see her long hair again, and here it was in my hands, wonderfully and carefully crafted into a necklace. She took it back from me and thoughtfully and slowly put it around my neck. She had a look as though she would never forget this moment, meticulously recording the event with her eyes and stamping each movement into her memory. She then placed her hands on my chest, my heart.

"This is a part of me," she said, "To always be a part of you."

As the train from Charlestown, New Hampshire to New York City bellowed its last call the following day, I waived goodbye to the ones I knew and loved. My mother sobbed uncontrollably, unconsciously tiptoeing along with the train as it pulled away. My proud father pulled out his handkerchief and inspected it like it was something else than what he needed it for, almost surprised to find it in his hand. My two older sisters half-heartedly waived goodbye, half-disinterested, turning as soon as they did, off to find adventures that involved more attention on themselves.

Then there was Mary, standing by herself just off the station platform at the edge of an open field. It was a field where we spent countless hours flying kites through the breezy and carefree days of our youth. Her arms were folded in front of her. She was as motionless as the air that day. I stared into her eyes for some time, as long as I could, as she did the same toward me, until a tree line close to the railroad interrupted our focus, and the just slightly turning autumn leaves extinguished the last image we had of each other. The train soon reached cruising speed, snaking south, paralleling the Connecticut River towards the greatest city in the world.

And just like that, I was out of Mary's life.

~

It was either the fourth or fifth step I took off the train at Grand Central Station when I collided with Plato, or rather brushed by him. His back was to me and although he didn't see me, he quickly sensed me, and stepped adroitly to the side the instant before impact. I, laboring at full speed ahead, too busy looking back at the heavy suitcase I dragged behind me, saw him at the last second, and, expecting impact, lowered my shoulder and leaned forward like the well-trained football player that I was. This resulted in me landing flat on my face with my suitcase crushing the back of my legs.

"My good man!" laughed Plato, "You move like a one legged porcupine in mud!"

He helped me up and brushed off the dust and dirt of the only suit I owned.

"Sorry," I blurted, "I'm not from around here."

"No doubt!" he said, laughing harder than before.

The enormous station was crowded with more people than I had ever seen, somehow making the giant room feel small. We were packed shoulder to shoulder and back to belly as far as I could see. At first I thought there must have been some commotion somewhere in front of us, perhaps an accident, or a police involved altercation, but it was none of that. It was just people leaving trains and catching others.

"I'm heading to NYU," I said, turning to Plato.

"Well! Believe it or not so am I," he responded.

"There must be a quicker way out of here," I travailed, looking for an exit that somehow no one else noticed.

"Agreed," he nodded, "Let's see if we can find one."

We sidestepped the crowd to one corner of the station. Plato found a narrow hallway that led us to what appeared to be a broom closet. We knew this because the sign on the door said so. We both sighed. As we were turning to trace our steps back to the lake of people, Plato grabbed my arm and whispered, "Wait a second."

He turned again finding the broom closet unlocked. Swinging open the door he flipped the light switch and indeed the small closet was full of brooms and mops and buckets. But at the back of this room was yet another door, half hidden from view by hanging towels full of filth and grit from the heels of the world.

"Where do you suppose that leads?" I said, straining my neck and eyes as if I could see through the solid door.

"I suppose it's worth finding out," responded Plato.

I shut the broom closet door as Plato opened the back one, and after stumbling over a mop and descending a flight of stairs I caught up to him, finding ourselves in a dark, damp and cold tunnel, as most by their nature, are. Plato went back and shut the door, darkening any vision we had of where we were and deadening any sound from what seemed like the billion people we had just left.

I became a bit uneasy, and although I could barely make out his silhouette in the low light, I could tell Plato was smiling. He relaxed his posture a bit, pausing to allow his eyes to adjust.

"Why is it," he turned, saying to me but as if thinking aloud, "that you suppose I'm so excited not to see people? Why do I find the world so wonderful when they aren't around?"

He followed with a soft laugh to himself.

"I can't say I can agree with you. Where we are isn't so wonderful," I said, looking myself over, checking for spiders and whatnot, "If I didn't know any better, I'd say that this was the devil's hideout or something."

Plato laughed. I didn't.

"It would be a good spot for him," he said casually, "Easy access to all the gullibles up there."

"Well, I hope it's not so easy an access for the ones in here," I retorted, "Is this some sort of abandoned subway tunnel?"

I imagined a train roaring through where we stood, but I observed no tracks or any sign of one ever being there.

"I was once interested in the selling of my soul but the devil was never interested in the buying of it," Plato said undistracted, "The devil is more human than we are. He only wants what he can't have."

We stood in silence for a moment or two, finally broken by another laugh from Plato.

"My good man," he said, "Did you forget to pack your nose in that giant suitcase of yours? If I'm not mistaken, we are standing in the bowels of the city. This is her sewer."

For someone I had met five minutes ago, Plato carried a confidence that distilled the fear in those around him. He had a calmness that was as easy to catch as the common cold. I was suddenly at ease, where I would not have been for a million years if I had been with anyone else.

"I think I see a way out," he said, pointing, and began walking to a light that came down from the ceiling a few feet from us.

Within moments we scaled a ladder, slid open a cover and were on the street as good as new, in the fresh air and sunlight, and on the better side of the crowded station that lay behind us.

"I'm Paul," I said, holding out my hand.

"Jonathan," he said smiling, shaking his hand with mine.

We took in the city and all of its beauty and filth and *busi-ness*. It just so happened that we were standing next to a man holding a large sign that read, "NYU Students"

I nudged Plato with my elbow, "Looks like we found our way to campus," I said, motioning to the guy with the sign.

"We are taught too much in life when we should be left to figure most of it out on our own," Plato responded through a chuckle, playfully brushing off the person with the sign like a mosquito, "There's no question we are dependent upon each other, but one becomes wise by finding the way, not knowing the way. What do you say we get there on our own?"

Surprised for a moment, I then furrowed my brow in doubt, but since he got me this far and since he had such a fun confidence about him, I quickly shrugged my shoulders and nodded in agreement.

"I think from here on out," I said without thinking, as if being hit on the head unexpectedly, "if you don't mind, I'm gonna call you Plato."

He shrugged his shoulders to me in turn, mimicking me with a nod and softly smiled with indifference.

If I haven't already, I will try not to bore the reader much further in describing Plato but will spend a moment here to round out his utilities. He stood nearly six feet tall with dark hair and was hued with a fair to medium complexion. He had an incredibly athletic build, especially for one who never played a sport in his life, and, just by witnessing the way he walked, one could tell he had refined control of his physical nature and potentiality. Over the years when we often ran throughout the city, sometimes racing each other from block to block and I saw him hardly break a sweat or become out of breath. These often occurred on hot days too. For the record, I never once won a race, even though I was an athlete on a well-respected and formidable college football team and was in the best shape of my life. Plato's physical abilities went almost unparalleled. There were athletes I played with, or against, who may have equalled his talent, strength, and perhaps gifted agility, but no one at this level who achieved it without wanting to, or ever really *trying to*.

One afternoon while he was waiting for me to get out of football practice, he spent the time talking to a pretty girl not far from the sidelines of our field. The practice soon ended and as a freshman it was my duty to pick up all the gear. In doing so, I decided to throw a football at Plato while he wasn't looking. He and the girl were across the field from where I stood, with his back to me and the girl facing me. I had a pretty good arm but it would take all that was in me to land the target which I had placed between Plato's shoulders. As soon as I launched the ball, the girl caught sight of it, and, soon realizing it was heading for them, gasped. Plato did not turn, but watched the eyes of the girl as it followed the high arch of the football. As the ball came back down to earth, almost at the bullseye of its intended target, with the girl's eyes tracing its trajectory, and Plato tracing the girl's eyes, he stepped slowly to his left, catching the ball at his side, between his elbow and ribcage, all the while with his back to me, without ever once seeing the ball until it was in his hands! He used the girl's eyes to catch the football!

To add to the astonishment for both the girl and me, he held the ball in his hands like it had been there all the time, spinning it in his palm, gently passing it from one hand to the other, talking to the girl in the same manner as he begun when he first introduced himself, as if the miracle had never taken place. He concluded the performance by turning toward the rest of my team who were just exiting the field, and, identifying my head coach, threw the football hitting him square in the back of his head, nearly knocking him over. The entire team and coaches turned at once towards me and my astonished face, and being speechless, I silently took credit for the bombardment of my leader, and ran sprints for the next hour and a half as penance.

Plato's physicality nearly matched the character of his person. He had a face that was smooth and calm but could be as engaging as seeing fireworks for the first time. When he talked, one could trace the lines from his mouth upward, never downward, in a restrained smirk all of their own; and beyond a few spoken words one could suppose, not just by sound but by even sight alone, that he was never sad a day in his life. His eyes never teared. His heart nor the wind never tempted them so. If it were not for that one time I saw him cry, I was quite certain that Plato never once did, not even as a child, or the day he was born; just from the demeanor of his contented face.

He seemed to say a lot of things without words. I imagined an expression in his eyes could inspire an author to fill the better half of a novel, or an ever so slight movement of an eyebrow could level a crowded room. Yet amazingly, not an ounce of arrogance ever surrounded him. There was a deep sincerity in his every action and reaction, whether it was his speech or expressions, or even in his laughter. His words, although written and read here could at times sound ostentatious and pessimistic, were overshadowed by his face and voice. No matter how harsh and cold the topic proved to be, his delicate and balanced presentation would always end with the listener feeling warmly and humbly educated. He was not remotely proud of his humility either, like some seem to be, who lift and throw humbleness about all day and still manage to perspire a subtle haughtiness on their skin. They often leave these stains in their clothing and in the air similar to a football locker room. No, Plato didn't sweat. He left no aftertaste of contradictions. He could almost pass as a walking definition of apathy, if used in its original and positive meaning.

He had a nonverbal yet whimsical temperament that simmered subjects. There existed inside him this reserved yet very evident fun-ness. It spilled out of his eyes and mouth and ears and fingertips. It remained fluid in any and every given moment, which seemed to further fuel his already extraordinary sense of wonder. Like a tornado trying to cower behind a chain-linked fence, it was a restrained energy that couldn't be concealed and always existed within the expressions his face produced, as if hiding in plain sight regardless of the nature or tone of the conversation.

Above this, there was an understanding within him that translated to those that he met. I closely observed people forgetting their desperation when around Plato, often without him saying a word, but silently replacing it with subtle excitement. Sometimes I wondered if he could be considered the closest form to gravity, where people circled around him with captivated obsequiousness, almost dependent on him for their existence. As far as I could tell, no one, including myself, was ever envious of Plato's life. We just wanted to be apart of it. We were timeless in his presence, somehow sensing the ages were irrelevant and insignificant, and, in a precious way, that we were, too. Of course I could never tell if Plato was aware of all this or completely innocent of the effect he had on others, but the outcome was always the same, and people often left Plato's company with better existences. More than once did I overhear them saying, "He understands me," or "He *gets* me." Despite the endless hours I observed Plato, it took me nearly the entire time I spent with him in New York City to discover what he was that most, if not all people are not: he was simply a great listener.

But there was a serious and slightly darker side to him too, a philosophical type demeanor that helped confirm his nickname. There were many times when we hardly spoke words for entire afternoons together, not because I didn't want to, but because he was so immensely absorbed and shadowed in private thought that it almost radiated from him.

One morning while we were sitting on a bench in Washington Square Park, a very young child ran around us, chasing a butterfly and screaming with laughter and excitement. He was barely old enough to walk, nearly falling several times while reaching for the butterfly that managed to stay just out of his reach. We both smiled as the boy's mother came and scooped him up, telling him to be nice to the butterfly, deterring his attention to herself, as she wiggled his nose and smothered him with kisses. The boy fell for her attempts, his eyelids half closing in contented joy, with a love that only a child and mother share. As they walked off together, Plato said, "That child's happiness is unequalled. It is perhaps the only time in life it is in its purest form. It is not earned, nor obtained by accident, nor premeditated, or fake, or contrived, or censored, nor is it acquired by luck or someone else's misfortune. I fear that I will never sense this joy without any preconceived notions or unconscious hopes of secondary gains. I am timorously concerned how fantastically jealous I am of that little boy."

The world became heavier at times for him, too. As I was complaining one day of something insignificant and now long forgotten, most likely involving my self-absorbed self, he interrupted me saying, "Sometimes, perhaps even on a beautiful and bright morning, I catch myself, if just for a moment, in a deep and severe depression. It's never an unhappiness focused on myself, but rather a striking sadness for *everything.* I can't explain it nor discover its roots, but the sorrow is so intense and unbearable that it is too sad for tears."

Unlike the rest of us, Plato never felt entitled to anything and seemed content to be wherever he found himself. He was someone who was simply reacting to the world he was in, but his way about it was always exquisite. Never did I detect anything calculated in his manner for nothing ever seemed to be planned. There was never the slightest hint of personal gain in any words or actions. His life was merely reactionary and reflective, and put simply, exquisite.

It seems as though when it comes to the whole scheme of things, no one really knows what existence is all about. There has and perhaps always will be a degree of uncertainty. Plato knew he didn't know and saw this illusion as really only just an illusion. With this attitude and secret knowledge, he appeared to others to be full of the wisdom of life, in which he professed to know nothing about. And so in turn, he was wise to others because he confessed he wasn't.

But I knew better of Plato. I would like to say that I was more acquainted with him than anyone. *He did know.* It wasn't because he said he didn't, or that he traveled the world or read more than a barn full of books. It was simply that, if for no other reason, he understood the wonderful potential of the human heart and the often conflicting and destructive power of the human mind; and in the end, his ultimate quest to improve upon both.

2

My first year at New York University was as much as I had hoped for. I expected intense challenges both on the football field and in the classroom, and my suspicions did not disappoint. I scarcely made honors my first year but improved on my grades slightly and almost consistently the entire four years I was there. School did not come easily for me and long hours at the library studying, even on weekend nights, were not uncommon.

As for football, I saw some playing time as a freshman and, like my studies, improved each year. I was never a star to be sure but I had pretty good games here and there throughout my career. I felt that the coaches were glad to have me on the team as much as I was glad to be on it, and that they had no regrets recruiting a somewhat small but scrappy kid from a very small and scrappy town in the little state of New Hampshire.

Within my four years there, the city of New York expanded exponentially, and was not so much growing out as it was growing up. The era of the skyscrapers was at full tilt and buildings were being erected almost overnight. At the same time there were bridges being built that helped connect us to the rest of America, and more importantly, them to us. It was also the beginning of the Great Depression across the nation with the stock market crash of '29, and, finally, to add to it all, the entire country was dry of alcohol, or so it claimed to be, as we were well into the years of Prohibition.

Hardly was there a dull moment in those days and like most throughout history I did not fully realize the times I was in. I knew excitement was around every corner, but most of the time I focused on putting one foot in front of the other. On top of all this, I had all I could do to keep up with the undeclared education by Plato. Perhaps the best habit I ever consistently performed was to keep and write in a daily journal. Almost every night after getting into bed I pulled it out to reflect on the day, and more importantly, I wrote down some of what Plato had said. My first entry is dated September 5, 1928: Plato: *A person well educated could perhaps roll off all the things that well educated people know, but I say, do you think you know you better than I know me? Are you more restricted by your mind than I am of mine? This is the primer to discerning observation; the first step of transcendence from the pursuer of wisdom to the possessor of it.*

I once asked Plato within the first few weeks of our friendship if he realized how smart he was. He responded by saying, "No one is smart, there is so much we can't help to be ignorant of, and since we are so immensely ignorant about things infinitely much more than we are smart about things, the world will never see a smart person."

When I countered this by having him compare his intelligence to others, he responded that anything he said or thought had already been said or thought of before, if not because of the limitations of the human mind and the thinness of its experience, then from the mathematical odds of peoples, mouths, and words. Real intelligence is originality, and true wisdom was simply knowing that one was *truly* ignorant. He added to this that what he had just said had also been said over and over before, and so on and so forth.

But Plato was heavily outlined with originality whether he admitted it or not. One fall afternoon we had rare company sit down beside us on a usual bench in Washington Square Park. The two young women were hopelessly and incessantly talkative to each other. After a few moments on our crowded bench, Plato leaned over to me and whispered, "Any person's best attribute is talking very little, or not at all. I'm ready to leave when you are."

And then, all at once, one of the women stopped talking and came down with a horrific attack of sternutation. She sneezed like a cat being stepped on repeatedly; and she who had to be her sister, sneezed in a similar fashion when she laughed. She apparently found the fits her sibling was having strikingly comical. By this alone one could tell they were related without any other attribute. But as the circus continued, it was hard to tell which one was laughing and which one was sneezing and drew such attention from bystanders and walkers-by that Plato and I snuck off unnoticed, sitting down on the other side of the park.

"I can't understand why silence isn't more popular," commented Plato, "It is one of the most neglected endowments of mankind. I don't know if I have anything more to say about what just happened."

"I don't know if I believe in God anymore," I whispered in reply.

Plato laughed.

"Well, I know I don't like cats anymore," he countered.

We exploded into fits of our own that day as the buildings west of us eclipsed the setting sun, signaling its light was soon to be extinguished.

As we got up to leave, Plato ended our visit to the park by saying, "Funny how you catch yourself enjoying a moment, when perhaps you might not aught to; and then realize how peculiar it is that you don't revel in these rare moments much more often."

These were only a few of the many talks we had and for the first several months of my freshman year, my eyes and mouth remained wide open from the things he said. But later on, I noticed that my mind began to open instead of my jaw, and I slowly started applying these thoughts to my own life and my own world. We would often meet up in Washington Square Park, for we both seemed to be drawn to the place, and Plato would often happen to be in that area for some reason or another. For nearly four years, I never quite knew what he was involved in on his own time, and never really thought to ask.

I adored Washington Square for I found a quietness and happiness to it much more than any other park in the city. As little as it was, it held its ground among the weeds of buildings that sprung up around it. A favorite among young families and the elderly, I initially felt like an outsider, but after only a few sojourns it was like visiting an old friend. I could sit on a bench there for hours without being bothered or could converse with Plato with little fear of being interrupted or overheard. Of all the things it was, I found it a perfect place to miss Mary. I devoted many hours there thinking of her. Writing and reading Mary's letters were almost exclusively dedicated to her here.

Indeed, there was a quiet contentment I developed when Mary and I were apart. In spite of the incurable sadness of separation, there was comfort knowing we existed at the same time; that we breathed at the same time. The world I experienced would not have been the same no matter the distance between us. We were both living; both full of life. We couldn't get entirely apart from each other if we had been on opposite sides of the universe.

Plato used to chuckle good heartedly with my pathetic-ness towards Mary, but he respected it. I resisted talking about her to anyone, but when he asked how she was, I shared my thoughts and feelings to him. Sometimes he seemed to have undivided attention as if he related fully to it (for love is so personal and universal), yet at other times, Plato acted as if it were something absolutely foreign to him and wanted to learn every detail about what and how it was. I thought perhaps it was probably one of the only times when I had something to offer Plato, where the teacher briefly became the student.

He did try to tell me that love was only desire, and desire was fleeting. I agreed with most of his take on human nature only because it made too much sense. But I somehow felt as though I was made to love only one person in my life, as if it were part of my design existing somewhere at the core of me. The idea of being with one person, being in love with that person, being the lover of only that person all of your life, can be wonderful. Indeed, the human condition, I fear, may not perhaps find it natural, but can find it and *make it* wonderful always.

I have had friends along the way like Plato, who have experienced many women, and some, unlike Plato, have boasted all too often of their ways. To be sure this may be only what nature intended. They were only playing their part, as does the rooster his hens. But being in love with Mary my entire life and experiencing only her was very natural to me.

I once asked Plato if he thought he would ever get married.

"I don't think so," he said, rather decidedly, "No, the love I've imagined to have for someone would exist far above the level of marriage. I'm afraid I've seen enough of marriage love in my life to expect any less."

"Do you mean to say that if I were to be married to someone I loved, it would be inferior to your level of love with someone?" I responded, almost offended.

"I mean to say that love often loses out to marriage, dear Paul, from what I've seen and heard in several ways. I keep a keen eye on it, and I've yet to find a marriage that proves otherwise, but I am willing to believe there are some out there."

I thought about all the marriages I knew at the time and frowned. Plato had a point. It did not deter me from my intentions with Mary, but I couldn't argue with him.

"Well," I said finally, "Jesus Christ apparently never married and no one seems to give him a hard time about it."

~

The inclined days began to quickly domino and when all but one or two badly tanned leaves had fallen from the hardwood trees in Washington Square, I met Emily for the first time. It was on a rare evening visit I took to the park with Plato. He said he had to run an errand or two, so I tagged along with the excuse for fresh air, but with an underlying and deceitful one of abandoning my studies. The sky was nearly cloudless on this cold November night. It was one of those subtle moments when one realized a season had permanently changed and there was no looking back to the previous one. Old Man Winter had set his feet firmly into the ground.

Plato had left me at a bench saying he would only be gone a few minutes. I took the opportunity to open a letter I had received earlier in the day from Mary. With the help of a moderate squint and the half light of the street lamps, I read her words with broad smiles and brief laughs. She was by far a better poet than I ever dreamed of being, which honestly and secretly bothered me. To make the matter worse Mary hardly took interest in this gifted and effortless ability. Every now and then though, she'd share with me a taste of her talent, like she did at the end of this letter:

So long the Sun so long are we
So far the Moon so close to me
You light my night and shade my noon
Sun of my heart, heart of my Moon

For the most part, I rarely felt lonely or homesick that first year of college thanks almost entirely to her letters. As I read them, it was almost as if she were speaking them to me, her voice as crystal clear as the first time I heard it, narrating her words as though she were behind me leaning on my shoulder and whispering them in my ear.

I sat there blissfully for a few moments thinking of her and her letter. As I finally folded it and put it back into my coat pocket, I turned my attention to the night sky and the ancient lamps that twinkled so abundantly. In spite of the artificial light from the city, the stars dominated the skyline like it was the only electrical source available. It reminded me of times in the not too distant past when this was indeed the case; when the light bulb was not yet a common household name, and the dark half of the world pulsed on instinct alone and not current. For some time I sat there motionless and wide-eyed, ensorcelled by the grandeur. I was reminded of the handful of nights back in high school when I snuck out of the house to meet up with Mary at our favorite swimming hole on the Connecticut River. We would float on our backs while holding each other's hand and stare up into the great dark blanket of the world, pel-melled with the timeless and never out of fashion twinkles of light.

"You know," said a sweet voice from the end of the bench I was sitting on, "those stars tonight are as bright as they are because of you."

I raised my eyebrows in surprise at both the compliment and her forwardness, and the simple fact that I was not alone. I could just make out her petite figure and dark, long hair. I crumpled my face into a puzzle, and then laughed.

"I suppose you are going to say they are a reflection of me," I said, half kidding and half insecure, slightly bowing my head in her direction.

"No," she said to me after a moment, returning her gaze up at the sky again, "They are reflecting off me."

I looked at her curiously for some time, identifying the beauty she emanated and the almost exotic way she sat, and wondered if she were real. As I was just about to ask her who she was, she said, without looking away from the sky, "You see, I simply lit up the moment I saw you."

My jaw opened slightly. Whatever remaining wisps of clouds were now gone and nothing existed but the stars and this girl. She rose from the bench as quietly as she had arrived there and said, still keeping her eyes on the sky, "Thanks for a wonderful evening."

She walked past me carrying a closed smile and large, evening eyes. The cuff of her full length coat just barely brushed the caps of my knees. As she left the park through the arch and disappeared up Fifth Avenue, I whispered to her silently, "What is your name?"

But she was long gone and so, too, was any sense in my mind.

"Who was that?!" said the almost breathless voice of Plato standing beside me.

I turned to see Plato carrying two large and heavy duffel bags over his shoulders.

"I have no idea," I responded, still stunned from the event, "She didn't say."

"Well," he laughed after getting a better look at me, "Come back down to earth and help me carry one of these things."

He dropped one bag from his shoulders into my arms. I felt like I just caught a train at full speed.

"Good God!" I complained, "Are we building another great pyramid with these blocks of stone?"

Plato chuckled as he adjusted the remaining bag on his shoulder, "No, we would need suitcases like the one you had at the train station when we first met."

"Haha," I sneered, matching his sarcasm.

We had almost made it under the arch, following the same footsteps that the wonderfully mysterious girl had made, when I had to stop and catch my breath. I dropped the bag rudely on the ground.

"I feel like a slave," I gasped almost seriously, "Is this not the land of the free anymore?"

Plato dropped his bag next to mine.

"In this society, we are all slaves to the idea of freedom," he said, with sophic interpretation.

We stood there in silence for a few moments. Plato had a way of interjecting and applying thoughts that often left those around him contemplative and speechless.

"Seriously," I finally said, pointing to the bags, "are there dead bodies in here or what?"

"Stop your belly-aching. I'll pay for a ride back to campus."

He hailed down a taxi and as I was getting in the car I looked back unconsciously to the bench for the girl, even though I witnessed her leave the park just moments before. The ride home was quiet and I could not stop thinking about her and the way she looked and walked and what she had said. What an extraordinary meeting! How eager was I to meet her somehow again. She continued to consume my thoughts in this manner until we arrived at our dormitory where Plato quietly and almost embarrassingly admitted to me that the two bags were stuffed with tens of thousands of dollars.

Generally speaking, when it comes to human events, we, as individuals, have the desperate urge to share a particular experience with others. We feel a need to tell of our accomplishments of success and personal gain. We want recognition for the things we do. In a lot of ways, we simply want to show off. I'm convinced that this society's mindset is not to do or buy or have anything purely for ourselves, but almost entirely to tell others of our achievement or purchase. Plato possessed none of these traits. As I dragged one of the bags to his room, he ended the night by stating, "I'm aware that there is no such thing as a secret, for a secret is only a conversation spoken in *softer* voices."

He winked at me quickly but then promptly toned his face into an expression that was dead serious, "The need for attention is beyond me. Tell no one of this."

And so I didn't, not even to Mary. I never found out how he acquired the money either until three years later when he left New York City. I tried to ask him once not too long after that night, but Plato promised me I was better off retaining my innocence and not knowing. As for the mysterious girl, we did not meet again until the next fall, almost a year later.

After concluding the cattle-chute semester, I finally made it home for the first time in my freshman year for Christmas break. Mary and I began where we left off, hardly missing a beat. My friends and family from the little town of Charlestown sat at the edge of their seats when I talked of my adventures of the past four months. They hung on every word like I had just returned from a corner of the universe.

3

My first winter in the city was an astonishingly harsh one. It was so cold that it was almost silly. I was very much used to winter weather, being literally born into it, growing up over 200 miles north of NYC, but the steel and stone of the urban tundra seemed to amplify the climate by many folds. Manhattan is surrounded by water and wind. The sea air whistles through the streets and ricochets off the buildings, almost increasing its energy instead of diminishing it. It was a hard coldness I never quite adjusted to. I still visited the park though in even some of the harshest weather conditions, reading and responding to Mary's notes and keeping a subtle yet keen eye out for the mysterious girl I met that previous fall.

Because of that first and unforgiving winter, it was I who turned the other cheek and forgave the season, for spring came to the city early and all at once. There were several weeks that I left my dormitory (after glancing at my desk calendar) layered heavily with winter clothing only to return later, carrying most of it under my arm. A week break from classes was coming up soon, as most colleges offer in the spring, and I was eager to return home. I half-heartedly asked Plato if he would like to come with me knowing he probably had already something much more exciting planned, but to my surprise, he said yes.

He had never been to New Hampshire but seemed to identify with it as well as I did. He was a true transient, blending in with his surroundings wherever he went. Mary greeted us as we stepped off the train and as a true New Englander, she was warm and polite to Plato but at the same time guarded and untrusting. There was an unspoken code of having to earn your *own lot* where we were from, and my new friend was no exception.

Naturally, this didn't take long for Plato, but Mary may have been tougher than most to convince. Perhaps it was because he was someone directly new to our lives, and, of course, anything new and unknown in human nature is considered threatening. But the ride from the train was full of enthusiasm and laughter and the three of us were as thick as thieves by the end of it.

Before reaching home, Mary said that most of the kids in town were at the baseball field scrimmaging and thought it a good idea to drop by and say hello to them. At the time, baseball was incredibly popular in our town, much more than football, and most children of all ages were out playing well before the ground thawed. So we decided to stop by to say our hellos. Not long after the short reunion, teams were chosen and baseball was being played. Plato politely sat out, excusing himself graciously as a better spectator, and watched with Mary from a small, three-tiered bleacher where my parents used to watch me in high school.

The field we played on was by no means official, with lines and distances between bases mere guess work, but it was a place where every kid in the area learned how to play the game, and even with a newer and fenced-in school field with straighter lines and more consistent measurements not too far away, this was always our field of choice, with everyone being drawn to its long history and legendary status.

The most celebrated part of this ball park lay just beyond left field. It was an old abandoned house, one of the first houses in Charlestown, that long ago gave up to time and mother nature, leaning horrifically to one side, missing its doors, most of its windows, and the majority of its roof. The side of the house facing the field had half a dozen windows, with each pane broken or missing from the hundreds of home runs the right-handed batters of antiquity to present day, took pride-filled credit for.

One famed window pane still survived though, toward the upper left corner of a second story window, hanging there glistening in its solitude. It had been the target of all right-handed batters in the town for decades, with not one kid blessed with enough aim or luck. When I was in kindergarten, a senior in high school reportedly hit the window pane with a home run ball, but it never broke or fell, adding unneeded fuel to this folklore of fire; the holy grail of our childhood.

A couple of innings that day had already passed when Harriet Smith, who, in her tender youth, was quite possibly the most loyal and dedicated disciple of the game of baseball in its entire history, before or since, stepped up to bat.

The players on both teams groaned light heartedly in unison. She was only nine years of age and all of forty pounds soaking wet but had developed a reputation of having a granite toughness that far exceeded all the other tough kids' toughness combined, times two. She had the heart of a lion, there was no doubt, but unfortunately had the ability of a newborn baby. In short, she could barely hold up the baseball bat, let alone swing it.

Harriet was part of the handful of families in town that was known as 'church mouse' poor. She and her siblings most often came to school barefoot because her family could not afford shoes. To make matters worse, the small shack they lived in had dirt floors and the soles of their feet were always as black as coal. The only exception to this was during the winter months where the snow and ice acted as an exfoliate and turned them to a slightly lighter shade of dark grey. I remember once during school I was caught staring at the feet of one of Harriet's brothers. I felt awful for it and turned bright red with embarrassment. He looked at me with a bit of confusion, not knowing what I was fussing and all uncomfortable about, not knowing how horrified I was at the sight of his feet and how sorry I felt for him. I suppose he knew his feet longer than I had, and he knew of no difference of how they could be.

A well-off husband and wife in town once took Harriet's family in for a few days to feed and wash them and tried everything and anything to remove the many layered black imbedded stains on their feet. But it was to no avail. The color seemed more permanent than tattoos. With much thought, the rich couple decided to buy the Smiths several brushes and buckets and soaps to take back home with them, and as charitable and thoughtful as their actions were, they could've saved money and had much more success with the option of simply buying them shoes. But sometimes, as they say, the more money gained in life, the more common sense is lost.

The first pitch whizzed by Harriet and was in the catcher's mitt before she started to swing. The plane of the ball was so far beneath and behind the plane of her bat swing that no one could comprehend what she was aiming at. Harriet frowned.

"Baseball is for boys," came a voice from the outfield.

Her frown disappeared.

"Say it again, I beg you," she yelled, "And I'll come out there and shove this bat down your throat followed by my fist!"

Silence.

The second pitch came in mirroring the first.

Strike two.

Harriet's frown lengthened and she backed off from home plate to focus herself. Her pride would not allow defeat even though the rest of her knew the next pitch would be similar to the first two. Just as I noticed the tears forming in her eyes, Plato got up from the bench beside Mary and walked over to Harriet. He smiled and then whispered to her as she nodded. He then addressed the rest of the field.

"Harriet has agreed to let me help her swing the bat as long as it's okay with everyone," he said with complete eloquence.

Not one person objected to the idea, amazingly enough, and so Plato positioned himself behind Harriet with his arms around her as they held the bat together. The next pitch came in quick and tight and so startled Harriet that she jumped straight back into Plato and the two of them fell over backwards with one on top of the other. Everyone laughed loud and hard, and Harriet wanted to beat up each of them but Plato calmed her down as he brushed off the dirt from her clothes and returned her to their batting position.

Now, as any seasoned baseball player or fan knows, the sound of a wooden bat hitting a baseball is a wonderful thing. Veterans of the game, even with eyes closed, can sense how well and hard the ball is hit, and have a good idea where it is headed after leaving the bat. A similar sound was made on the next pitch to Harriet Smith, and those that had ears had no question what kind of hit it was.

The baseball seared off the bat like a meteor in a flat and straight line toward the old house beyond left field. Upon impact with that last and most celebrated window pane, the ball blazed through the glass like a bullet, leaving an almost perfect circle in its wake with splintered cracks to the four corners of its wooden frame. The ball could be heard ricocheting within the second floor of the house for several moments, finally coming to rest in some unknown and unvisited room of darkness.

And at that very same moment, a legend was born. The holy grail had been obtained.

Complete silence concussed the earth. The spectators to the event could not pull their eyes off the broken glass, each wearing similar faces of disbelief and confusion. Everyone there knew they were witnessing history, but couldn't quite process what had happened.

The earth began to spin on its axis once again as a faint cry from home plate was heard with Harriet Smith collapsing helplessly upon it. The poor child's body fell onto the ground like a paint splatter. Her sobbing was profound and unrestricted. The players and bystanders rushed to her in an instant but once finding her at their feet did not know what to do. She was still the toughest kid in town, and if they tried to help her up, or simply console or even congratulate her by patting her on her back, in spite of the momentous occasion, they still weren't sure if they would be hugged or punched. The muted crowd seemed to turn their eyes toward Plato, who was already closest to her, down on one knee and holding her hand.

"Harriet," whispered Plato after a few moments, "I'm not too sure of the rules, but to make it official I think you have to run the bases."

Harriet was somewhere else at this moment. She was star high, consuming ether, soaring too unconditionally free to notice the little world beneath her. Indeed she was crying, but seemed to be in a wonderfully deep and sound sleep of cataleptic bliss. An historical event occurred, and she was the unexpected and fabled star of it. The sobbing continued incessantly, interrupted only by coughs and sniffles her sweet and joyous emotions created. Plato was quiet for a few minutes more, then finally said, "Maybe I could help you?"

A faint nod of Harriet's head was barely perceptible, at which Plato gently picked her up, cradling her like an infant in his arms. She buried her face into his chest.

"That was a beautiful hit, Harriet," Plato said as they headed toward first base.

He walked the bases carrying Harriet in his arms the entire way. The rest of us all watched in silence. I could see him whispering quietly to her as they went, as she responded with a subtle nod or shake of her head. Just before reaching home plate, Plato lowered Harriet down onto her feet and she slowly and unsteadily made the last step on her own. She wiped the tears and dust from her eyes with her sleeves, all the while staring at that home plate between her shoes, which now was her promised land, her very own Shangri-la. She turned to Plato and threw herself into him giving a big-hearted hug. Then, all at once, she raced off towards left field, pushing the crowd out of her way as she did.

Harriet retrieved her home run ball from the house, holding it close to her heart with both hands as she appeared at the front door. She glanced over at us for a split second then jumped off the front porch of the poor old house and ran toward town without looking back.

~

After deflecting credit for the first half of dinner later that evening, Plato politely asked my family to drop the subject of the now famous home run that the entire town was buzzing about.

"For the record," concluded he, "I was looking the other way as the pitch came in and when Harriet swung the bat, I had all I could do just to hang on."

Those of us at the table, including my two sisters who were batting their eyelashes at Plato the entire evening, accepted his answer but didn't believe a word of it. Plato then turned toward my father.

"Mr. McNamara," he said with smiling interest, "Who is that mysterious botanical philosopher you have as a neighbor?"

The table drew faces of confusion on all of us. No one in town came close to fitting his cryptic description.

"I'm afraid you'll have to be more specific," said my father, almost more dumbfounded than the rest of us.

"The woman next door here, Mrs... Mrs. Tharrow? What a fascinating person."

"You can't mean Mrs. *Sparrow*, the old spinster?" my father said, flabbergasted.

"Yes, that's her name. I'm amazed at how many clever people there are out there in the most unexpected places."

"She's crazy, not clever," said one of my sneering sisters.

We all knew very well that Mrs. Sparrow was considered the harmless town lunatic. She always kept to herself and hardly ever left her house, and when she did, was seen talking to people that weren't there.

Plato gave my sister a face of confusion similar to the one we had given him just moments before.

"That's not what I gathered," said Plato with a smile, "I stepped outside just before dinner and saw her watering her garden, so I walked over and said hello."

"But it's pouring rain outside!" said my other sister pointing out the window.

The table erupted in laughter. Dark clouds had indeed rolled in a few hours before and the rain had not let up since.

"What's more," added Plato, "She was watering a part of her garden that was completely barren and full of rocks."

Everyone at the table laughed harder, including myself.

"Is that what you call clever where you come from, Plato?" I joked, silently realizing I never asked where he grew up.

The dinner party laughed some more at which Plato patiently took in stride.

"Well," responded Plato, "Naturally, I was thinking the same thing and brought it to her attention. Without looking up from her garden, she said to me, 'The clouds won't bring enough this time so I'm helping them out a bit. This part of the garden, like all of us every now and then, needs to be reborn.'"

Plato paused, reflecting on the neighbors words for a moment.

"Taken somewhat aback," he continued, "I said to her, jokingly, 'Why, as much as I adore when it rains, it's too bad you have to water your garden while *in it.*'

"She stopped watering at this and stood up straight. Turning to me she said, 'Rain often ruins plans, spoils picnics and glooms faces as well as skies; this has been so since the first human felt the first drop on his head. But if one listens closely enough and sits still long enough, the pitter-patter of raindrops on a leaf or a rooftop, or the palm of one's hand can softly bring about a happiness that no other fair weather employment can afford.'

"I took a full step back from her," continued Plato, "almost unconsciously, to acquire more room to process her words and found no other response than to nod in agreement.

"'How peculiar it is,' she then added, 'that the human forces who shove this world around in circles, have never been based on wisdom. Emotion has never lost a battle to reason, nor ever will.'"

The table grew silent at these words. Plato wasn't finished.

"I then said to her, 'I agree. Emotions are ignorant, but necessary. Perhaps I also expect too much of the unexpected and in that way, I've been unexpectedly compensated by my expectations. But you don't suppose that there are any plants in this part of your garden, and if there were, that these plants could ever come back from the dead?'

"To which she responded, looking at me straight in the eye, 'I suppose *anything*. It matters not if one is imprisoned or free; smart or dumb; sick or healthy; poor or rich; at war or at peace; blind or can see; happy or miserable; alive or dead, sane... *or crazy*. What matters is *knowing the difference*. I wonder, do you think you are not dead? How many people do you know who are alive?'

"'Well, I'm not quite sure,' said I, stalling as I attempted to understand her razor-sharp meaning, 'But between the dead and alive I can tell the difference by the amount of complaining that comes from their mouths."

"'Ha!' Mrs. Sparrow laughed, 'If complaining were a profession, we would be the most prosperous society the world has ever known! That goes for excuses too! By God, if I had a dollar for every excuse I've heard!'

"'Yes,' I concurred, 'I'm afraid the Gods of Contentment rarely visit this world.'"

"And then Mrs. Sparrow said to me, 'I've yet to see any God in this lifetime or the others I've had before. The eulogy of mankind was delivered long ago, but everyone forgot to bury themselves, and no God will call upon the dead. Pray tell me, you aren't from around here are you.'

"I told the woman that the only place that matters where one lives is in here," Plato said, gently tapping his head.

At this point, the entire dinner party was leaning in towards Plato as if he were holding something very small in the palm of his hand and we needed to get a closer look. But it was his words that drew us in of course, for his hands were empty, yet they moved slowly and methodically to the sound of his voice, almost synchronizing with the motion of his mouth. Forks and knives laid still on the table. We were captivated.

It was almost as if a winged messenger had come down through the ceiling and joined us for dinner, and although the language of heaven has yet to be determined, this particular one spoke in plain English, and we hung on his every syllable.

He seemed to be followed down by yet another, smaller angel, that carried a bow and a quiver of arrows, who shot both my sisters square in the heart, and, I'm almost embarrassed to say, my mother as well. I would not have been surprised if the small angel may have grazed Mary with an arrow too, perhaps nicking her in the arm, barely breaking the skin, from the look of interest I observed in her eyes as she sat motionless beside me.

I then looked at my father who was deep in thought at what Plato had said. I had so much respect for my father in so many ways, as I was most like *myself* when I was around him, and considered myself mostly like *him*, and to see him so impressed by Plato made me feel, in an odd way, proud. Although he denied ever reading or writing a word, my father was a sage in his own right, on a grounded level, a hard worker who knew how to provide, build or fix all the necessities of life; or could figure it out on the rare occasion he came across a problem he hadn't seen before. With much complaints from my mother, my father helped his neighbors, townsfolk, church, friends and strangers in so many different ways, from replacing a motor in a car, to raising a barn, to installing plumbing or electricity in their houses, to planning the town of Charlestown with roads and buildings. There seemed to be no shortage of men from all over that came to him for advice or help. As for myself, until the day of my father's death, there was not one time, in the entire history of me, that I did not become a better person after spending time with him.

And here he was, amazed at the insight of a person more than half his age that I brought home from college for a few days, and discovering from him a neighbor he never knew he had.

My sisters, Irene and Dot, remained skeptic about the neighbor.

"I still say she's crazy," said one, as the other nodded in agreement.

"Perhaps it is wise to get to know her better," responded my father.

"At the very least," said Plato, "She's a whistler."

The dinner party became confused once again.

"What I mean to say is," Plato continued, sensing the ambiguity, "she is a happy person. I don't know of any sad or angry people who whistle. Your neighbor was whistling loudly and unconsciously when I walked over to her, and when I asked her what tune she was bellowing, she was taken aback at the suggestion, and with a playful but honest look on her face she replied, 'Was I whistling?'

"How odd and wonderful the art of whistling is," continued Plato, "and I have discovered that it is always and entirely performed by the light-hearted. What a merry soul Mrs. Sparrow must have! So overjoyed it must secretly exhaust from the owner its merriment through a straw-lipped musical instrument, nearly deafening to others but mute to its player, if only not to burst!"

Plato then laughed at the idea of it all.

"We simply have far too much to learn from those who whistle," he concluded.

I looked around the table to see that I was not alone with my facial expression, for my family smiled quietly and thoughtfully along with me.

"I once won a contest in high school for being the best whistler," blurted out my sister Irene, batting her eyelashes more than ever and thoroughly ruining the moment.

~

It wasn't until we boarded the train back to New York that I had a chance to replay the entire incident when Harriet Smith hit the home run of all home runs. Or rather, Plato hit it for her. As the train sat waiting in the station for the last of its occupants to climb in, and we had said our long goodbyes to my friends and family, and Mary, I sat down to transcribe the incident in my journal.

I happened to look over at Plato across the aisle from me and noticed he was busy writing something too, perhaps a letter. I don't think he realized the impact he made on my little hometown. He would never know the effects of breaking that windowpane far off in left field and how it broke generations of hearts and dreams with it too. He stood time and place on end for those of us who grew up in Charlestown. He couldn't possibly be aware of all that. One pitch, one powerful and smooth right-handed swing, and one never forgotten hit.

I thought of all this as I stared at him scribbling down on some paper in his lap. As his pen moved purposely across the paper, one last thing I realized that nearly made me double over in my seat and stood the hair up straight on my arms: Plato was left-handed. He hit that home run as a right-handed batter.

The train then finally began to creep forward, and as I was about to acknowledge Plato's dexterity with him, a scream from outside was heard.

"Plato!"

It was Harriet Smith. She was running after the train as it slowly staggered away from the station. I lowered my window and both Plato and I stuck our heads out and waved enthusiastic goodbyes to the now famous little girl. She waved back for a split moment with one hand, and then she raised her other hand high above her head, holding in it the baseball that broke the celebrated window pane. With a quick smile and nod, she twisted her small body almost to the ground, and with all her might, uncoiled herself and launched the ball towards us. Plato nearly jumped half way out of the window to catch the ball with the end of his fingertips, and after pulling him in I looked back at an ecstatic Harriet jumping and waving and laughing and crying.

We soon lost sight of her and the station, and I sat back down to catch my breath. As I was shaking my head with a smile, trying to digest the excitement of the last few days back home, Plato showed me the baseball. It was covered with different colored crayon-drawn hearts and read, "*I will never forget you Plato, love HARRIET.*

~

The remainder of my freshman year at NYU that spring of 1929, dragged on, for the weather continued to be beautiful, and I longed to be somewhere else other than where I was. But before long, I was once again stepping off the train to a place I knew as home, and Mary was once again there to embrace me as I did.

I said goodbye to Plato back in New York. He had plans of catching a ship to Europe, perhaps, to explore for the summer, but he wasn't quite yet decided. He was equally interested in another ship he knew of that was headed toward South America. I told him to flip a coin, to which he agreed upon, as well as a promise to tell me all his adventures to where fate had sent him, upon our reuniting in New York City in the upcoming fall.

Like the summer before, Mary and I took advantage of the time we had. We spent most of it in our bathing suits, swimming and fishing and canoeing; and exploring the coastlines of both New Hampshire and Vermont on the Connecticut River. To be sure, it was perhaps no Europe or South America, but we didn't feel like we were missing out on anything, not for a second. We were happy as clams that we were in our own backyard and, above all, that we were together.

Upon a small hill that lay just above our swimming hole, was a tree that Mary and I used to climb together. I can't remember which one of us found it first, but it was a perfectly shaped and fat-waisted maple stuffed full of branches; large limbs shot out from its trunk just inches from the ground and continued consistently in the same fashion to its top. Sometimes, we would sneak up there to eavesdrop on those swimming below us, who were always ignorant of our presence; but mostly we would go there to become unknown and hidden from the world.

We often climbed as high as we could, usually perching ourselves against each other as we sat on a limb or against the opposite sides of the spine of the tree, and wasted several summer afternoons as such without care for responsibility or time. More often than not while on those top branches of that beautiful tree, Mary would sing to me. She wore a very subtle smile when she sang, as if she were almost trying to suppress the joy she was feeling. With the aid of the gentle breeze that always seemed to be waiting for us there, and with the multitude of maple leaves that surrounded us, they, as did I, would rustle in delight at the sound of her soft and delicate voice.

This was my favorite place in the world. Our position gave us magnificent views of the river, both from which it came to where it was going, and we were just tall enough to catch the green mountains of Vermont to the west. On a few afternoons we stayed long enough to see the sun set behind them, and only one or two times did we wake early enough to see it rise from the mountains of New Hampshire from the east. Nonetheless, it was the only place we felt as far away from the world as one could become and simultaneously had by far the best view of it. There was nothing more comforting and tolerable than sitting atop that big shaded maple tree.

Only on extremely rare and special occasions there, I, too, would sing to Mary in turn as she leaned her head against my shoulder with one of her hands brushing away every now and then the hair that tried to flank her dark blue eyes; while her other hand, softly yet firmly, held mine.

Impossible though it seemed, the endless summer ended, proving quicker than the previous one, and I found myself once again saying goodbye to Mary at the train station. Her last words to me there were soberly and indistinctly prophetic.

"Make time go faster," she whispered after kissing me on the cheek, "I almost got used to being without you."

I took a half step back from her with a tilted head and a look of bewilderment.

"I won't ever get used to being without you," were my last words to her.

4

As my sophomore year began, I noticed a slight yet sound change in nearly everything about me. Situations on all matters recruited less desperation. This especially held true with football. I found that my competitive nature had diminished, where winning and losing didn't seem to matter as much. Certainly I still loved the game, but I didn't play to win anymore. I played because I loved to play. At the immortal and ripe old age of nineteen, my insecure desire to rule the world was slowly but inescapably fading.

Of course I had a hinting suspicion that this was due in some part to Plato. It was a quiet yet emotional solace to see him after he showed up nearly three weeks late into the fall semester of 1929.

"I was beginning to think you weren't real," I said, with a slight sigh of relief, after exchanging big smiles when he appeared in the doorway of my dormitory room.

"I'm not," was his response.

Plato got delayed in Spain, he proceeded to tell me, along the coast somewhere in a small village that didn't show up on the map. I asked him jokingly if he were really escaping from a girl's father of some prominent and rich Spanish family, and for a split second he gave me a look as if I had been following him.

"It's good to see you, Paul," he said laughing in such a way that completely erased his previous presumptive look.

Whether I realized it or not, it was refreshing to be around him again for many reasons, if for nothing else but to parallel his take on life. By catching up with him and hearing about his adventures in Europe, I felt that I was recharged and anew, for I may have harmlessly returned to my old ways of thought a bit over the summer. But nothing appeared lost on him or myself in our three months apart, and I was hungry to transact more of the rawness of existence with him.

"When is your last class tomorrow?" Plato asked me, as he began to walk out of my room.

"My last and worst class is Philosophy," I lamented, "I should be done by two. And since tomorrow is Monday, it's my day off from football as well. Why?"

"I am meeting up with a friend at a bar for a drink and didn't know if you would like to tag along."

I was later surprised at my initial reaction of jealousy from what he said. The idea of Plato having acquaintances other than myself to spend time with, hit me abruptly, for in a strange way I wanted to keep him from the rest of the world; only because I had so much more to learn from him, even knowing all the while that the rest of the world was equally in need of him too.

As I walked into my Philosophy class the next afternoon, I was greeted with a wave of a hand belonging to Plato, who was sitting comfortably at a desk toward the back of the room. He had saved a seat for me and motioned me over. With a look of bafflement on my part, he responded, "If you don't mind, I would like to see what this class is all about."

"Suit yourself," I laughed.

My teacher was a man in his early fifties, and was as dry as the subject matter that was being discussed. He tended to pause a lot in the middle of sentences for no apparent reason, producing very awkward moments, sitting on his words and sentences like they were satin cushions; procrastinating on each one out of pure indolence and arrogance; outstaying his welcome to human language and thought as well as to the class in front of him. In turn, my classmates and I carried quizzical brows more from this than the topics themselves, and so the education hardly transferred.

"Today, we will begin discussing the writings.....of Henry David Thoreau," stated the teacher with his back to the class, wearing a suit and tie that was a size too small.

I rolled my eyes in boredom at Plato, but he gave me no reaction.

"Who here can tell me about him. Has anyone read him?" he continued.

My classmates were as interested in the writer as much as I was, and no one answered. Finally the teacher faced the class and scanned the crowd. He settled his eyes directly on Plato.

"You there," said the teacher, "Are you assigned to this class? You seem unfamiliar to.........me."

"I am not," Plato confessed, "but I was hoping it would be okay to sit in just for today?"

"I suppose," granted the teacher, almost offended by not being asked for permission before class started, "As long as you can tell me a bit about Thoreau."

Plato leaned back in his chair slowly and folded his arms.

"Well," began Plato, "I have read him and still do. But I'm afraid I don't like him."

My classmates awoke from their comas at this and turned their heads toward my friend.

"Phhh," responded the teacher, now even more offended, "Perhaps it is because you don't understand him, like most of the world?"

Plato smiled. "No," said he, "It's not that. I simply despise Thoreau for stealing all my thoughts and beliefs I never knew I had within me."

The teacher's reaction was interesting. At first his facial reflexes appeared disgusted and was deemed ready to retaliate with a derogatory remark, but he caught himself in mid-thought, stopped, and raised his eyebrows to the top of his head.

"Well now," said he, "Not.....bad, not bad. And, tell me, what exactly do you despise in him most? His views on slavery? Materialism? Government? Conformity, perhaps?"

"Nah," Plato said, "It's probably his views on the self, and the reliance of it, for I can't think of any other way now to exist."

"Well, well, well," commented the teacher, who was now respectful in tone, but also tried not to reveal enlightenment of a student, "If, perchance, Thoreau appeared in this classroom today and saw the world as it is today, what do you suppose he would think?"

Plato laughed, "I can't say, but maybe it would be something about having too many philosophy teachers and not enough philosophers."

The teacher laughed self-consciously in response but regathered himself quickly. A couple of students toward the front of the room snickered softly.

"Tell me," insisted the teacher as he refocused, "what do you think Thoreau would say was the biggest human catastrophe or blunder in our history, that has made us the immoral and self-important animals that we are?"

"That I cannot say either," said Plato with a slight shrug of his shoulders, "But if you were to ask me the same question, I would say, without having an exact date, that it would probably be the very moment we acquired consciousness."

On the cab ride to the bar, Plato briefly described his friend Copper to me, but when I met him, his metallic name was far too soft for his being. His demeanor was more like iron or steel, as was his frame.

"Paul," I said, with a nod introducing myself, as we sat down at a table he occupied.

"Copper," was his flat response.

Without any other knowledge, I could tell there was a toughness Copper possessed that I had never seen before. It was no act. His composure was in such a way that one knew instantly not to mess with him. He was not loud, nor did he carry a scowl or puff out his chest. He had a quiet, unbreakableness that you did not want to test. His bluish-grey eyes, perhaps more charcoal in color, were his tell-tale sign that gave this away. One acquired an uneasy yet unmistakable fear when looking into them.

To be more specific, if a gang were to have come through the door to ransack the bar and everyone in it, they would pass on Copper with one look, even if he were outnumbered 10 to 1, leaving him quite alone and beating the guy next to him to a pulp. Or, better yet, since we were in the days of Prohibition and bars like the one we were in were actually illegal, a wagon full of police officers came barreling in with batons and guns and handcuffs, I felt as though they wouldn't lay a finger on him from the fear he instilled from the back of his eyes.

But those same eyes ever so slightly brightened a bit upon seeing Plato, as most eyes do, and Copper and I then had at least one thing in common, which, in a strange way, made me feel a bit less insecure around him.

"How ya been, Plato?" said Copper, with almost a faint hint of a smile.

"Oh, I still believe I will miss this life if there proves to be another one, for it seems on occasion I catch myself missing it already." responded Plato, almost indifferently and with more of a smirk.

Drinks were ordered and I almost missed the fact that Plato told Copper his nickname as if it were his real one. I suppose he didn't want others to know too much about him, which suited him perfectly, but I was naturally as proud as a parent to hear it, being the one who gave him the moniker.

"Have you been able to track down the thing we talked about?" started Plato.

"No, but I'm on it, and it shouldn't be long now."

Copper motioned to the waitress for another refill of his drink, and I thought my eyes were playing tricks on me for all of us had just ordered our first round, but he seemed to be a bit thirstier than Plato and I. In fact, he ordered 4 or 5 rounds for himself before I took two sips of mine and before Plato had even touched his glass.

Copper turned out to be a person who could get things, any thing, for anyone. Being born and raised on its streets, he knew New York City from head to toe, from the golden glitter parts of it to its guilty gutters. He was an infinite source of information and materials, but what separated him from the rest was his refusal of any monetary benefit. He couldn't be bought or sold, for money disinterested him as much as it possibly could. Therefore, I thought silently of him as the Robin Hood of Manhattan, only a lot tougher, trading one deed of an evil for a deed of goodness and vice versa, as though he outlined the historical behavior and justification of all humanity.

As I was thinking just this, Copper reached into his pocket and pulled out a fistful of cash with his very big fist, and threw most of it on the table.

"Well boys, I gotta go. I'm late for church." stated Copper as he stood up from the table.

I was, as if in a comedic play, in exact mid-swallow of my drink and nearly lost all of it, for I thought it a joke; knowing Copper as little as I did, expecting anything from his mouth other than *that.* But with one quick and serious glance from him, I knew he wasn't kidding, and all function in my body, including my gag reflex, stopped, and I sat there like a statue, speechless.

"Would you two like to go with me?" he added.

I began to slowly nod my head up and down, coming up with no other conceivable answer due to the fear that entered every cell of my being, until Plato chimed in.

"Thanks Copper, but I think Paul and I will sit this one out," said Plato, "As for me, I'm afraid all religion has lost my interest, even the harmless ones. They all increase the falseless-ness of self-absorption and delusive importance, and the good Lord knows that we've got enough of that in our makeup without religion adding insult to injury."

Copper's eyes thinned as he stared at Plato.

"If I didn't know you, Plato," said Copper finally, "I would have torn you to pieces ten seconds ago. Since I do know you, I'm still thinking about doing the same, but we can talk about this later."

Copper then emptied his large glass of brown and neat liquid, placed it firmly on the table and walked out without saying goodbye.

Plato raised his eyebrows a bit, "I'm glad Copper knows me," he said.

"Amen," I whispered.

Plato then described more about Copper to me. He said that he would rather fight than eat and drink than fight. A good day for him was when all three took place. He alone wished to live on the latter two, but needed fuel for the furnace that snared inside him, and, more importantly, that provided power to land a closed hand on its target. He never once started a fight, but always was known to end them. Drink only cloaked his fear; not the kind of fear that one has for fighting, for that long ago disappeared in Copper during the days of his youth. It was the dark fear that nobody talks of; that all men carry with them; and that which is temporarily atoned by other means. This all, of course, was carried out with Jesus by his side, whispering in his ear, showering Copper with approbation and reverence for his actions.

Minus all profitability and glorification, I thought Copper was a wonderful example of man's condition belonging to any war-raging nation: worshipping some sort of God with some sort of drink; and leaning on both for vindication.

Soon thereafter, the bar became quite crowded and loud. Plato and I much enjoyed the atmosphere, so we decided to migrate over to the bar when Plato noticed two empty stools at the end of it. We still had the same two drinks that we started with, half of mine being miserably forced down, while Plato still hadn't had a drop of his yet. We talked and laughed as the afternoon turned to evening, keeping to ourselves like we were on a bench at Washington Square Park.

"Consciousness is a fiction," Plato sighed, perhaps alluding to my class earlier in the day. And then he sighed again, "But so is reality."

"You talk funny," butted in a blonde sitting next to us, wearing too much make-up, leaning over towards us at the bar, eavesdropping in her coquettish way.

Plato smiled, already aware of her.

"Perhaps," he said.

"Well I like it," added a brunette, wearing even more make-up, who sat on the other side of the blonde, as she leaned over her light haired friend, "Say something else."

We stayed there most of the evening, disinterested in the two girls which naturally made them more interested in us. When we got up to leave, the same girls just happened to decide to leave at the same time, as coincidence is so rare, and followed us out. As I was exiting the bar, I glanced over to a table next to the door and noticed my football coach sitting close to a young woman that wasn't his wife. I quietly motioned to them after making eye contact with Plato. He smiled and shook his head,

"Consciousness is contradiction," he laughed.

Because of my family indoctrination of good manners, I instinctively made a gesture to my coach to say hello, but Plato quickly grabbed me by the shoulders and re-directed me through the front door without saying a word.

The fresh air out on the street was more than welcomed to my lungs and, instead of haling a cab, I decided to take the long walk toward home, alone. Plato headed in the opposite direction, with the blonde and brunette, as they hooked themselves around each of his elbows vying for his attention.

But only a few blocks later, as I started to cross a street, I nearly jumped up a lamp post in fright from a gentle tap on my shoulder. The finger belonged to Plato and, after witnessing my reaction, he leaned his head back expressing a noiseless and contagious laugh, followed by a wide and even more infectious grin.

"I thought maybe we could walk up along the river for a bit?" said Plato, after I gave him a few fake body jabs for scaring me, "Have you ever really watched a dark moving body of water at night?"

"I can't say that I've ever remembered to notice it in such a way," I admitted, "Those girls wearing too much paint on their faces for you, eh?"

Plato gave a quick laugh.

"Perhaps it was I who wasn't wearing enough," he replied.

After a few leisurely blocks west we reached the Hudson River, or as the natives once called it, "*Muhheakantuck.*" Plato told me this word meant a river that flows both ways. It all depended upon the direction of the tide. The source of his endless knowledge of little comments like these, I had yet to discover, but it was always interesting to hear. He was also exact with his earlier description, as we stood there at the edge of the river staring into it, almost hypnotized by its tar black hue and untethered velocity.

"Whether a lake or river or ocean," Plato observed, without turning his eyes from it, "There's a sense of home when near water."

The clouds above us were moving fast for the almost still air we found ourselves in, as well as heading in the opposite direction of the river, which made the water appear quicker by the reflection.

"Why is it that there's a small part of me that desires to jump into that water knowing that I would probably never survive?" I said with no direct correlation to his statement.

"There's a cheerless side to us all, but wanting to discover the unknown seems to be a strong and strange human trait, even when it comes to death," was Plato's reply.

"I guess I keep forgetting that I'm not going to live forever."

"What's worse is trying to accept that nothing is forever, not even this river."

"What you said in my class today..."

"Ah," Plato said, politely cutting me off, "I shouldn't have said anything. The professor provoked me and I fell for it."

The river muted our conversation and Plato fell into his well identified look of absorbed thought. He soon picked up a small stone and threw it as far as he could across the river, reminding me of that football throw that hit my coach's head. At the time I felt bad for my coach, but after seeing him tonight I figured that perhaps it was well justified.

As Plato scanned the New Jersey shore line, he gave out an audible sigh and almost unwillingly said to me, "It's just that I'm not quite sure consciousness has a place here, and I'm pretty sure humans were not ready for it the moment they obtained it either. There is no doubt I am in complete awe of it and its infinite, immortal thoughts that end mortally, but consciousness has a funny way of clashing with everything. It is such a wonderful and rare weapon, that often wages war on itself more than anything else, and in either case is its own ultimate demise."

We fell silent once more. The river was the main attraction tonight and it drew us in again, as its darkness silently slithered by us at thousands of gallons a second.

"I have never questioned," continued Plato after a few moments, "if I was made of this earth, this clay. I've wondered though, if our ancestors were from some place else."

Plato twisted the ball of his left foot on the hardened mud that framed the river.

"Even so," he continued with a shrug, "our existence is always worth making the most of. Breathing, it seems to me, is still a wonderful concept."

"So should we just continue to complain about our ability to complain?" said I, finally contributing to the conversation.

Plato turned to me with a respectful look of acknowledgement.

"You sound like your neighbor back in New Hampshire," he said with a smirk.

Without another word or gesture, we both turned from the river and climbed back up its bank toward the direction of campus.

"Say, what has come of all of that money you acquired last fall?" I asked, as our walk planed out on the smooth and civilized sidewalk and we hit our travel strides.

"Oh, I suppose I gave most of it away," confessed Plato.

I then confronted him on why he did so, and he responded indifferently and very simply by saying, "I discovered that I had little need for it."

After returning to campus and saying goodnight to Plato, I found myself most effortlessly awake after crawling into bed. I sat there propped against my pillow, wide-eyed and sleepless well into the night; so much so, that I noticed I hardly blinked. There, for some time I stared out my little dormitory room window and into the cloudless night looking for any signs of nocturnal life and watching the stars, as they were so kind to blink for me.

Perhaps the day's events helped contribute to my condition, but I was a child in adult clothing; in silent wonder of the universe; without any detail unnoticed; every object new and brilliant, as if I were *un*-blinded; and had just acquired sight and was able to see for the very first time.

I hope not to ruin this with words, but these nearly extinct moments make all the rest of it more than worthwhile, no matter at what horrible degree the rest is, and if only a handful of these occur in a lifetime, I dare say it could last me several.

5

During the Fall of 1929 with youth as my catalyst, I was absorbing life like a black hole, inhaling anything in my path or within reach, harnessing more energy with each experience or insight that occurred in my daily existence. Football season was now in full swing, as were my studies, but these felt like side jobs to me compared to the *employment of life*, and I devoted every possible waking hour to this demanding and full-time work. I was on such a high from it that I hardly noticed Mary's letters arriving later and later as each week passed, and their content being more distant and less invested, until one day Mary ended one by stating, "*Perhaps we should take some time off from each other?*"

When I read her letter I was at Washington Square and in a rush, and it didn't quite sink in. It wasn't until I was a few blocks away after leaving the park when the words slowly materialized. I pulled out the letter to read it over and over again, trying to understand it, thinking that it would end differently each time. In a panic, I began to run, almost haphazardly, looking for a phone to call home. I finally got her mother on the line but she told me that Mary wasn't in and wouldn't be for some time.

Not far up the block from where I was walking passionately and still aimlessly, I spotted Plato across the street talking to a man outside of a grocery. He was eating an apple and laughing with what looked like the store owner. For only a moment I felt a slight relief.

"I need to see Mary," I said loudly and to the point, as soon as I reached him.

Plato didn't challenge the look on my face. Understanding my desperation immediately, he reached into his pocket and threw a small and shiny projectile at me. I caught it instinctively just in front of my face and discovered as I opened my hand a set of keys. I looked at him quizzically and more frantically.

"Behind you," he said, with a faint smile.

I turned to see the biggest and prettiest and shiniest car in the entire city.

"Whoa," I whispered.

I then looked back to Plato and was amazed that he was talking once again with the man just as he had been before I had rudely interrupted them, as if he had just waved hello to me as I was passing by. I was somewhat offended he wasn't half invested in my emotions as much I was, but remembered the quote he told me recently by Thoreau: "In what concerns you much, do not think you have companions..."

After quickly forgiving him and his disinterest in my dilemma, Plato finally glanced over at me and saw that I was now carrying a look as if to say, *'Where on earth did you get this?'*

He gave his quick smile with a subtle lift from one of his shoulders.

"Copper," he replied, "Go find Mary."

The extremely brand new 1929 Cadillac V-8 Dual-Cowl Sport Sedan felt like an extension of my body and responded almost as quickly as my thoughts. I was out of the city in no time carrying a heavy foot and a heavier heart; heading north as fast as this wonderful machine would take me, in hopes to resuscitate the only love I had ever known.

I couldn't have snuck away at a better time. Mondays were our days off during the football season and if all went relatively smoothly, I would arrive in Charlestown by nightfall that evening, have a few hours to talk with Mary, and then drive through the rest of the night to make it back for my first class the following morning. My calculations were not too far off, for I turned onto Main Street of my hometown just as the sun was setting.

It was an awfully odd feeling driving through my little town without anyone knowing I was there or having any inkling that I was supposed to be. I was entirely unknown in this fancy car, and although it was somewhat of a late hour, a few people were still out and about, walking their dogs or each other, making the most of an unseasonably warm autumn evening. But in spite of my real purpose of being there, I felt an esoteric liberty or immunity because of my state of anonymity, and although it was a very serious night, I caught myself smiling because of it. It reminded me of how Plato once told me, "*The only hope for any real freedom is to be unknown.*"

I finally turned onto Mary's street and slowed the car down considerably as if I was in a parade. My senses were on full alert upon reaching her house. As I was looking intensely after noticing a faint light emitting from her bedroom window, a loud bang from the front of the car nearly deafened my hearing, as well as all of my other senses. My foot instinctively stood on the brake pedal.

"Watch where you're going you moron!" screamed a man's voice as he lifted his hand off the front hood of the Cadillac after slamming it down hard and with authority. But my attention was quickly diverted to his other hand, for it was doing something more damaging and sickening all on its own. It was firmly holding the hand that belonged to Mary.

The two crossed the street to her house as I watched them with shattered eyes. I could faintly hear a short giggle from Mary as he pulled her closer upon reaching the doorstep, and my foot unconsciously released itself from the brake. My hand desperately clutched the necklace around my neck that Mary had made me two summers ago, and the car slowly pulled away from the scene, preserving its disillusioned driver's identity, and leaving his heart on the street where the love of his life had lived.

As those who have experienced similar events understand, the hurt I felt on the ride home was infinite. Countless times did I want to turn the car around and confront Mary, or, find the guy she was with, but the roaring Cadillac kept its nose headed south. For the first time in my life I wanted to be alone.

By the time I arrived in the city my hurt was raw. It had slightly become tinged by anger too, as most heartbreaks on the short end are, and I immediately wrote Mary a note responding to hers, mailing it on my way to class that following morning. As I let go of the letter into the mailbox, I experienced a strong urge to follow, mailing myself to Mary along with it. I walked off stuttering under my breath, as I repeated over and over the cryptic note aloud. I only wrote her three words: "As you wish."

On Mary's behalf, a few days later I received a letter from her expressing heartfelt apologies, and that I didn't fully understand her, and what she previously wrote to me wasn't exactly what she meant, and so forth. She didn't necessarily want us to end, but thought only that it may be good for both of us to take a break from each other. Perhaps, thought she, it might even be healthy for us.

I was still too badly broken and not remotely ready for any type of healing to begin, and with a surprised shock to my stubbornness, her letters went unanswered, as did her phone calls.

A couple of weeks had passed and my heart and its tributaries remained starved and *transi de froid*. I found myself at Washington Square with every spare moment I could find, sitting away hours with only my thoughts and exposed pathos. I brought with me neither paper or pen, or letters, or anything to distract the determination of engulfing myself completely in the feelings of the moment.

It was there, on another almost Indian summer day in late October, that the clouds broke and the sun shown bright and warm on me and the bench I was sitting on. I could feel my shoulders and neck warm in obsequious delight as my face gleamed of gratitude toward this giver of life. The sun stood itself tall in the sky and somewhat behind me, so I leaned my head back to let it have a better angle upon my face- like a star worshiper, or like sunflowers are known to do. Once establishing a comfortable position, with arms stretched long out to either side upon the top of the bench, and legs crossed lazily over one other, with my face now tilted so far back that it almost pointed in the exact opposite direction in which I sat, I remained there motionless as a statue and as mindless as one, too.

With its endless ability as an artist, the human eye often finds little else more attractive or interesting than itself. We often adore the mountain views or the night sky with respect and awe, but nothing seems to stop us in our tracks more than an unexpected reflection of ourselves. Sometimes though, an object can come into focus that can make its own vanity forget itself for a moment or two. For me, this object was Emily.

As I sat there silently worshipping the sun, an otiose wind walked by and a shadow eclipsed the light for an instant before I felt a warm and full mouth place itself upon mine. The kiss, or more like an upside down kiss, came from behind, with the plush pair of lips surrounding my bottom one, fitting quite naturally, quite perfectly, departing all too soon and leaving me wanting more.

When my eyes finally opened from this extraordinary sun-dream and I discovered who I was and where my surroundings were, I jumped up and looked around somewhat nervously to see if somebody witnessed it. I instinctively looked for Mary, since her lips were the only pair I had ever known, scanning the entire park and beyond, but she was no where to be seen. My eyes finally fell on Emily, who was now sitting where I sat, as content as a tiger after a large meal. She said to me, quite frankly, more to herself than to me, "So far, that's the best kiss I've ever had."

I stood there awkwardly and speechless, unable to process the moment, with a look on my face like I had just awakened in a strange and unfamiliar place. Emily noticed my condition, rolled her eyes and tapped on the bench beside her for me to sit.

"Oh stop it. No one saw anything," she said with a giggle.

I did as she requested and we looked each other over for a moment in silence. Emily had so many wonderful parts to her that it was impossible to take them all in at once. She had the smallest and most delicately sized wrists and ankles a girl had ever worn on her person, and if she possessed no other trait of attraction, she would be sought after remorselessly by those blinded by beauty for this attribute alone: with a subtle flick of her wrist, or an unconscious tip-tap-toe dance of her foot as she sat with a leg crossed over the other, as she did now, swatting away with her hand a silly sentence playfully spoken in mid-conversation.

But her hair was what drew the innocent from afar, being sculpted onto her head like some sort of medieval statue, only thicker and darker, with significantly more influence and suggestiveness. In a perfect light, it almost appeared wet; as if someone dipped her head into a barrel of motor oil as a cruel joke, and as a by-product created a Greek Goddess with a mane that billowed like heavy black smoke down over her shoulders and onto her hips. Her hair had such feminine confidence to make any potential suitor clammy with sweat in her presence, and if she happened to possess an empty core of a personality, which she did not, her soot black locks would have carried her through the most intelligent conversations recorded on the planet without her saying a word, all the while having heavy influence on the subject discussed at hand.

This is no exaggeration. Her hair moved with the rest of her body in a way that anticipated each action and almost led her body in a particular direction instead of following it; and as so, quite naturally, how men followed her. When I was finally able to pull my eyes away from her centripetal pull, I noticed a man at the other end of the park staring over in our direction with body language all too obvious; pleading extreme and hopeless interest in Emily. Other men, both young and old in the neighborhood, fell victims as well, as they were innocently going about their day. Young couples with babies in strollers walked by, where fathers tried their best not to deliberately gawk, while mothers simultaneously exposed instinctive looks of hatred toward Emily for her very existence, somehow being terribly offended and threatened that she was in the same park at the same time as they were.

Whether wrong or right, it is no secret that beauty trumps all. Women, if they don't already, could rule the world with very little effort, or no effort with very little and well-positioned clothing. A man's thinking is no more pathetic than when a beautiful woman comes into view, with his actions proving just as profound. That moment of recognition reveals nothing is more serious or important; nothing more useful; the Fates laugh incessantly at the overplayed joke and Eternity always turns her head in defeat.

All this and more was Emily. I, admittedly, drooled over her from afar, but wanted nothing to do with her when she was close. I was far too guarded and imprisoned with my heart; reluctant to admit that it still and always belonged to Mary. Without having that investment in Emily though, I could happily watch the circus that was created around her for hours on end and witness how envy and lust and other deadly sins played out over and over again in her name.

"What's your favorite smell in the world?" she finally said as we grew more comfortable on the bench with each other.

"Well now," I said, after some serious thought, "if it weren't for some of my mother's cooking, I'd have to say it would be chimney smoke from a wood fire on a very cold and clear winter night."

"Hey, that's my second favorite!" screamed Emily, with eyes full of energy that were almost too big for her face.

We sat there exchanging likes and dislikes, and ideas and hopes that only the young have; losing track of time because time didn't matter, because time was a play toy for the children we were. It was well past midnight when we said our goodbyes and Emily leaned in to kiss me goodnight. I stepped back from her before she could and whispered in an apologetic tone, "I'm sorry. I can't."

She smiled with a look of understanding, grabbed my hand and quickly kissed the back of it instead, and wonderfully walked off under the arch of Washington Square Park again like she had done nearly a year ago.

It just so happened on the very next day the stock market crashed, and New York City almost instantly became cold and hungry in both appearance and character. Mary and I continued to remain cold as well, starving ourselves from one another, and even though we did see each other when I returned home over Christmas, it was in a paralleled universe. In just a few short weeks we had become complete strangers. Neither of us seemed to be despondent of our situation, but we were playing entirely different and foreign lives from the ones we had always known. When I visited her family one evening I remember being oddly uncomfortable and out of place. Her parents were warm and polite as always, but appeared to be as uneasy and unsettled as I was. Perhaps there were things they knew of Mary that I didn't, and worried that I would put them in a position to tell me, or, would be forced to lie to me for the sake of protecting their daughter. I never asked anything in that regard, and to save them from any more unspoken agony, I did not return to their house again over the holidays, even though I promised I would. I left for NYC without telling Mary goodbye, but I still looked for her at the train station. It was then that I realized after boarding the train and staring back onto the train station platform that I had never felt more alone in my life.

Lucky for me though, I had a wonderful distraction named Emily, and as I stepped off the train at Grand Central Station, she was there to greet me. As promised, I had sent her a quick note from New Hampshire when I planned on leaving, and I arrived back in New York City just one week after the new year and subsequent new decade. Emily was all dolled up like a first class traveller, wearing a smart green dress and a matching hat that tried in vain to hide that wonderful mane of hers. We had indeed become friends since that late

October day just over two months ago, and I confess that I was pleasantly surprised and happy to see her there welcoming me back in all her deference.

"May I take your luggage for you, sir," she joked in a low and manly voice, curtseying as she did in her brilliantly perfect and coquettish way.

"Shut up," I said with a laugh as I looked her over, "I wonder, how did you get such a pale name with such dark and exotic features?"

She crinkled her nose at me in playful annoyance and grabbed my hand as we walked toward the exit.

"I was named after my grandmother if you must know," she responded, "And she was whiter than a ghost! Even so, I was never much fond of my name, that is, until you said it. Happy 1930!"

Emily, like Plato's friend Copper, was a child of Manhattan, and the noise and cars and people never recruited a second thought to her world. As I held on tight to her hand, she spear-headed our way through the station and out onto the street as if it were empty of people, when it was almost as crowded as the first time I had arrived there, the very first time I met Plato.

"Well," said Emily, as we were standing on the sidewalk looking for a cab like the dozens of other people who surrounded us, "For the record, I've fallen for you. I've missed you so much since you were in New Hampshire that it hurt. There, I've said it."

She then shrugged her shoulders and followed it with a hint of a humorous sigh as if glad to get it off her chest. I smiled at her with a bit of a shock on my face but said nothing.

"Don't worry," she said after feeling my silent and uncomfortable expression, "I realize you have stuff going on with someone else and that's okay. I just wanted to let you know how I feel."

"Gosh," I finally said, stumbling the word over my teeth and gums, "I'm honestly flattered."

And I truly was. Like the rest of the men on the street, I couldn't get over her flawless figure in that little green dress. She was so well put together from head to toe that it was almost numbing, and I had trouble pulling my eyes away, and once I did, they unconsciously returned to her not too long thereafter. So quietly astonished was I by her beauty, but what amazed me even more was what she ever saw in me. I had literally no business being with her.

"It was the first night I laid eyes on you," she began, as if reading my mind, "I watched as you read that letter, and how you laughed, and smiled, and read it again. You have a wonderful composure about you. There is a calmness in your eyes and mouth. I knew almost at once you were from some sort of distinctive and singular stock."

She gave out a short giggle to herself, remembering the moment before continuing.

"You see, Paul, I often look for my soul to have the wind knocked out of it. I want it to be jarred. I want it to lose its footing. Up until that night it never had. With you, it did."

There was a calm energy in her eyes that wouldn't allow my own to look away from them.

"Aannnd," she said, drawing that one syllable word out with her smile, "What *did me in* was when I heard your voice."

I laughed instinctively, for she had an unrehearsed funniness about her. She was quick and clever and quirky, which only furthered her legitimacy as the perfectly wrapped gift that she was.

"Well," I said laughing, with a silly face of my own, "I think you are not right in your head, for I can hardly believe that any man could deserve you, let alone me. But since you've been so forward, please allow me the same liberty."

Emily nodded with restrained enthusiasm, but I soon lost the smile on my face and looked her straight in the eye.

"The truth is, Emily, I think you are wonderful in every way. If I had an image of a perfect person to be with, it would, without any hesitation, be you. I can't find one single thing wrong with you, not one, and good God, how I've tried! But my heart is tethered to someone else who is more a part of my life than I am, and even if I never see her again, I will always be attached to her - and no one else. It's something that cannot be broken and I feel empowered and powerless by it. So don't waste your time with me. Find another who, although won't ever deserve you, will at the very least give you all of his heart."

Emily looked down at her feet with the last line of my soliloquy. I only stood there staring at her, waiting for some sort of reply, but none came. I finally looked down at the curb of the busy street corner as well, and closed my eyes. The crowded street with people yelling for cabs was only a soft white noise to my ears. But then, a searing pain started in my stomach that pushed back quickly and forcefully to my spine. Emily had punched me square in the gut.

"Nice try, Paul McNamara!" she yelled with a devilish smile, "You think I'm just going to give up that easy, eh? As heartsick as I am from your words, I will, at all cost, persuade you otherwise! Who do you think I am? Give up on you? Ha! Never!"

As I was bent over with both hands on my knees trying to recover from her forceful blow, she grabbed my arm and led me through the crowd of people, parting them like Moses did the Red Sea. She reached a cab with a door to it already open, shoved me in it, smiled flirtatiously and thanked the startled man who hailed the taxi down, and climbed in with me, giving me a big long kiss on my cheek.

"Just so you know, there's more where that came from," she continued, without any sign of giving up, "I warn you, from here on out, I'm going to kiss you whenever I can, when you least expect it!"

She gave me a goofy smile, crossed her arms and looked poutingly away from me. I said nothing because there was nothing to say, but mostly because I was still having trouble breathing from her knuckles to my midsection. I could only sit there curled up in the back of the taxi cab as it sped away from the teeming corner. I was in such pain from this little tiny girl, but it didn't have a chance of erasing the smile on my face that went from one of my ears to the other, and, while bent in half and still clutching my vitals, I found myself at eye level with Emily's perfect little ankles that were ever so slightly exposed beneath her perfect little dress. I couldn't stop thinking how I had no right being in the same world as she, let alone the same taxi cab. The only remote answer I could come up with was that I simply said no to her and her heart, and that this was perhaps the first time she had any experience with such an answer. In turn, this gave her a dedication that wouldn't have been there otherwise, and the hunted, as rarely as it occurs, became the hunter.

And yet conversely for me, there was within my sounded thoughts a craziness at the idea of resisting her advances when no mortal *could* or ever *would* dream of doing so. It would have never been entertained by anyone else, even in hindsight. Yet my entire being was quite insulated and encapsulated by Mary. Our souls were soldered in confected alloy and even though she shattered my heart, she still held all the pieces. It just so happened she forever would.

But at that moment it was all smiles: smiles and a hurting stomach. There in the back of that vehicle that raced through the city of New York, I felt as though the world was mine for the taking - only because I didn't want it; and the wick at the stem of my mind had never been alighted with a larger nor hotter flame.

6

Plato encouraged me to spend time with Emily. He, too, thought her a spirited distraction, and sometimes the three of us would explore the city together, or spend an afternoon or two at Washington Square, but most of the time there was only two of us, and mostly it was Plato and I. Of course I instantly thought that Plato and Emily would make a magnificent pair and although they got along tremendously, laughing and flirting with each other, and ganging up and teasing me often, the relationship never seemed to materialize. If there were anyone who could give Plato a run for his money it would be Emily, and, quite equally, so, too, was Plato for her. Perhaps I was just barely enough to be in the way and in some small regard I regret thus being so.

Warmer days arrived once again and like most people in the northeast, I was complaining about how hot the weather was right on the heels of how cold it was, without any downtime in between. But warm weather meant another year gone by and one morning, with just over a week left of classes of my sophomore year, I awoke with a reserved fright that I was halfway finished with college and halfway closer to the realities of the real world.

As much as I couldn't wait to go home, I had disquieting reservations of returning because Mary and I hadn't spoken with each other for some time. Although my home town was as much mine as it was hers, I almost felt like an outsider to it and in a small but traitorous way I wished to spend my summer somewhere else.

Later that same day I met up with Plato and asked him what his plans were for the next couple of months. He was undecided about his options, but since he went to Europe last summer, he thought he would venture to South America; this time by default and stow away on some cargo ship leaving out of New York Harbor.

I then asked if I could tag along with him, like a gag reflex, inviting myself like an annoying friend, not believing the words that came out of my mouth, nor even having a remote idea of what I was getting into. To boot, I also had almost no money to my name, with no potential source of any financial assistance from anywhere or anyone.

Plato calmly watched my facial expressions as my mind ricocheted these thoughts and when he felt I was quite finished he said, as if hearing them, "That's the best idea you've come up with, dearest Paul. I will agree to it on one condition, that any expense throughout the entire trip will be covered by me and only me, and not a penny will be found on you, unless given by me, without any thoughts of ever paying me back."

Of course I refused the offer, but he insisted on it being the only option permissible; which I finally relented to, ending the agreement by promising I'd make it up to him someday and somehow.

I telephoned home to my parents to tell them of my summer plans and although I was over 20 years old at the time, I respectfully asked permission if I could go on the trip. They seemed excited for me almost more than I was myself, which in turn made me much more eager to partake in the adventure. When finally on the phone by himself without my mother listening in, my dear father quietly offered to send me some money down for the trip, even though I knew he had little more to spare than I did. I respectfully declined, realizing historically I always took from him the money he would offer, as little as it sometimes was, even though it was often the last dime on his person. I felt a cold chill with this enlightenment and at once discovered I did not deserve him as my father. Without question he was the most selfless person I have ever known. To cover my tracks a bit, I made up a quick lie to him that I would work my way through the trip, which ended up being almost entirely true.

As we were just about to hang up, my father said to me, "Oh, and tell Plato hello for me and that I've been talking with our neighbor quite extensively and learning some amazing things from her."

"I will, Dad," I said with a laugh, "Plato will be pleased to hear it."

"Good. Thank you. Oh, and one last thing, I'm sure you already know, but what a paralleled coincidence that Mary is leaving to work on a cruise ship this summer bound for the Bahamas. Perhaps with any luck you will see each other in passing."

I was somewhat astonished at hearing this, for Mary was more of a homebody than I was and seemed quite content with her job since graduating high school as a phone operator in town. But perhaps she wanted to be somewhere else for once that season also and to be away from the summers her life knew all too well. I only wished I was somehow involved in her plans, if only for an afternoon.

Plato and I met up one last time at Washington Square before leaving for the summer. He had just gotten all the information about the ship we would call home for the next three months. Although I had blind confidence in Plato and his ability to get all the things required for traveling halfway around the world, my parents insisted on at least knowing what ship I would be on, and so I copied this information down to be mailed up to New Hampshire before we left.

As we sat there on our usual bench, the birds in the park sounded more excited to be in NYC than we were at the thought of leaving it, singing at the top of their voices, belting out melodies that all but drowned out the usual noises of the city. I was still very much uncomfortable with Plato footing the bill of this trip. There was no doubt he was well aware of my *dolour*, but I felt like I had to discuss it again with him.

"I just wish I had more money for this, Plato," I lamented, as we sat on our bench watching the birds swoop around and whiz by us on their merry way. "For that matter, I wish I had more money for everything. Life would be exponentially better."

Plato made no immediate reaction to my comment, but I noticed that well known smirk cloud over his face and form on his mouth as his eyebrows lightly danced with each other, playfully hiding the thoughts that gathered behind them.

"I'm not sure you are ready to hear this Paul, but I hope someday you will understand it," he said, with a respectful yet amusing glance at me.

"It seems to me," Plato said, without looking at me, "After thorough and exhaustive thought, that life has to be, for lack of any better or more original description, a travesty, and rarely a good one at that. It applies at any time, to all levels, even the sad and serious parts, for we play the same prank on each other and ourselves over and over; pretending a brand new emotion is felt in the very first way, at a very first place, for the very first time, and that no one has ever experienced before in the entire world. Of course it is not for me to admonish any experience from anyone, but most act as though they themselves are the initial persons to ever have one and that no one else ever has. I'm afraid perspective appears to be long extinct in this world."

Plato intertwined his hands and placed them on top of his head with his elbows pointing out to each side as he repositioned himself on the bench before continuing.

"As such," he said, "We do seem to get a lot of things wrong. Our arrogance with greed, for instance, is as funny a sin as pride. The people I know with excessive wealth consistently act more poor than I am. They never spend a penny and scream bloody murder when forced to. The dust piles high on their high piles of money, and so too does it settle on their own shoulders and heads and eyes and ears; and thus their senses are clouded and dulled and their money owns them more than they own it, and the shot across the bow that tells us that no one owns anything is stubbornly ignored. But they insist on hoarding their gold as if they will live forever, or at the very least can take it with them when they die. Some live their lives as meaningless as the piles they keep in their worthless, soulless, pride-filled vaults. Two of the deadly sins here covered, not bad."

Plato shook his head with a sighing yet simple laugh. I knew Plato well enough not to interject anything to what he was saying, not that I had anything to say, but because I knew he was just getting started.

"Instead of acting poor," he continued, "be poor. Existence is a mindset. Burn your money. Don't spend it. Don't give it away. Let us all desire to be paupers together. Let us all desire only the needs in life and none of the wants, for that is the only real success. Maybe then we will have a chance at contentment. Let the paper money take the chill off come colder months in your fireplace. Send a smoke signal to others of your cherished *dis*-fortune. Only then will it be truly useful."

Plato then shifted himself to face me and looked me straight in the eye.

"For the most part, I've been surrounded by a people with an income that could just afford the necessities of life- which is all one really needs, and also a lot more than most in the world have- and the only thing worse than the rich who act poor are those at this level who think their lives would become infinitely better if they had just a little more money, or certainly, a lot more. Most people are *exhaustively* misguided. They are not satisfied in the position they are in and think there is always someone else who has it better; and this makes their lives continually worse. Those with superfluous wealth are innocently penalized for not having to concern themselves with the necessities of life, creating a Brobdingnagian void, and in turn complain and worry of petty and inconsequential daily activities of themselves and others, placing a much needed shave and a haircut on the level of urgency in order to save the universe. And so the joke's on them of course; a bad one at that. Sadly enough, I am not only humored by the rich, but to a much larger degree, I pity them; so too for those who dream of and seek superfluous wealth and fame, as there is little hope for their kind. To own is to be owned, and along with the fear of losing that which is possessed, *one loses oneself.*"

Plato half laughed and shrugged in his usual and almost indifferent way, but I could tell this subject bothered him more than he was leading on and further troubled his quiet hurt for the world.

"Sorry," he apologized, shaking off the subject in disgust, "Less fortunate are we in the things that matter and too fortunate are we in the things that don't. Unless someone is starving, I get offended by anyone who thinks money solves life. Personally, I'm always astonished how happy I've become from all the things I never had. But alas, speaking of sins, I daresay if one were to take the two I've mentioned and add in the clearest and most literal commandment, one would have a soldier. What a fear driven employment misdiagnosed as heroism! I wonder, was there really ever a Christian other than Jesus?"

"Okay, okay," I said, half confused and half in awe, "So humans are bad. Maybe I should just wish for world peace then?"

"World peace," said Plato with a frown, "is very dependent on human extinction. One will never occur without the other. Thus it is why I've allowed the great answers to stay just out of reach. I know they will not apply. How limiting it is to know the correct way and at the same time know it can never be!"

As for me, Plato was right in saying I wouldn't quite understand. In time though and perhaps to a lesser degree, I would begin to understand, but it consequently and embarrassingly took many years to do so.

Emily said goodbye to me at my dormitory. I had just gotten out of the shower and was only half dressed when she showed up in my doorway unannounced.

"My God," she gasped, "You have a delicious figure. It's damn near perfect."

She then ran at me as quick as a cat and jumped on my back, kissing me on my bare shoulder and embracing me with all her strength.

"You know," I said, trying to wiggle her off me, "If you weren't so beautiful, I would have you committed to some mental hospital for evaluation, but since you're irreconcilably breathtaking, I suppose I'll keep you around. There must be some severe correlation between beauty and madness."

Emily slid off me and slapped me on the butt, still checking me over.

"I just can't believe I'm letting you go for the summer," she said smiling, shaking her head, and making a *tsss, tsss* sound with her tongue and the roof of her mouth. And then, as if changing gears all at once, a sadness emptied onto her face and she began to wipe her eyes.

"Try not to fret," I said while putting on my shirt, "If it's like any other summer I've ever been a part of, it will go faster then you want it to. Besides, I'll write you as often as I can."

"It's not just this summer," she said with little energy, "It's the thought of our time altogether; and how it is quickly coming to its end."

I went over to her and gently held her by each arm. We then hugged for some time without saying a word, with the calming silence only being interrupted by Emily's most heart-wrenching and adorable sniffles.

~

The morning we were to board the cargo ship, I sent out a letter to my parents as promised, but with it attended another one to Mary that I included below:

Your heart is my church.
What it holds is my religion.
You, Mary, are forever my Savior.
And although it cannot be now
I miss everything that once was.

Tell me, teach me, to forget.

Paul

Decades later and a few weeks after Mary had died, I was going through her things and found this same letter in the bottom of her favorite little purse with the chickadee embroidered on it. She managed to keep the letter in perfect condition as if it had been written that very day; and I, holding it in my hand, felt as though I hadn't given it to her; and by some strange instinct was impelled to mail it to her once again.

7

Leaving New York Harbor reminded me of the first time I left on the train from New Hampshire to Manhattan. Once again, I was heading to an unknown world and there was a nervous energy within me that I couldn't shake. It was also the first time I saw the city as a whole from a salt watered point of view, which gave me a better and grander scale of it, as well as a lesser and more insignificant scale of myself.

My sea legs, thinking that I already soon and soundly obtained them, were tested not too far after our departure, as we were off the coast of the Carolinas when we ran into some inclement weather. It was well into the darkness of night when the waves grew from the black confusion like weeds in a garden, appearing upon us in places they weren't wanted, but nonetheless, they, being like any dominant power of any given region, invited themselves over without asking. I was so amazed at the immense energy in the ocean. Despite the monstrous size of the ship, I was also bewildered at the intensity of my sickness from its rocking and tossing. I couldn't tell who had more of an upset stomach, the sea or me, and so I resigned to curl myself up into a ball on my sleeping hammock, trying not to move a muscle for what seemed like a lifetime. As Plato did not fare so well either, though much better than I and the sea, it proved to be the only time I regretted going on the trip. Early that next morning I wrote in my journal to remind me of the moment: "*Surely the world is priceless; so too is the life found on it, but when one is sick and in bed trying endlessly to find sleep and wellness, it is not worth a damn.*"

As soon as we lost sight of land, I lost perspective as well. This was the first time I was on an ocean for any considerable amount of time, and although I could hear the roaring engines beneath me and the gentle head wind on my face, it felt as though we were running in place. If someone told me we were anchored and at a standstill I would have readily believed him.

Our captain was a specific and quiet fellow and nothing of the sort I pictured a captain of a ship to be. He appeared very young to me, baby faced with a pearly-white complexion, that somehow had been sheltered from the harsh weather of wind and sun the open sea had launched at him his entire life. He ran a very tight ship and the crew appeared to admire him greatly, for never once did I hear a bad word said of him. He also loved stowaways, oddly enough, welcoming us aboard before we had a chance to sneak upon it; treating us like distinguished guests, and although we were put directly to work to earn our keep, the captain would often lower himself to our level, spending long afternoons with us talking and lying around on the wooden crates that littered the deck. He turned out to be the type of captain that wasn't afraid to get his hands dirty, often being seen performing jobs about the ship that only the lowest of deckhands were required to do. He was laconic yet easy going with us and his crew, which in turn demanded respect from all, which, in turn again was equally given back by him.

Ol' Cap, as we called him for he *was* the captain and *was* so young looking, told us that he ships pretty much anything that demands to be shipped, mostly about the Western Hemisphere. On this particular trip around South America, the entire cargo was chockablock full of Schwinn bicycles. The world demand for two-wheeled transportation had taken off at this time and Ol' Cap was the Santa Claus of summer, handing out these toys at each port like it was Christmas morning, as we skipped down, around, and up the coast of the southern continent. Of course, we opened a crate or two along the way, with Ol' Cap's permission, having intense races with the other crew members by circling the deck's perimeter. The hooting and hollering from these events, as well as the insatiable competition they produced, still mark my memory, and never had I witnessed a group of grown men more infested with the powerful will to win; and upon winning, celebrating as if they had just won a lottery, or a world war, or had entered heaven itself; or, upon losing, becoming so distraught and depressed that they were literally ready to throw themselves off the ship into the depths of defeat. Friends became enemies in an instant and fights nearly broke out from some of the finishes that were too close to call. Plato shared his observation of this little sport and applied it to the rest of human life, and how people must always have an opponent and how all of us have the pathetic and silly desire to conquer.

"As true as it is said for a God," he concluded, "So too as it is for an enemy. We must have one, and if we didn't, we'd have to make one up."

Besides this obsessive pastime and the coastal cities we briefly visited, there were mostly large doses of solitude aboard ship, with Plato and me being left all to ourselves on this enormous vessel that carried less than twenty souls. Moreover, I found myself without Plato for huge chunks of time, as he, in his preferred state, enjoyed time mostly with himself. It wasn't long before he noticed my innocent agitation of having nothing to do, as boredom mixes so well and quickly with youth, and so called me out on my disposition.

"Paul," he said light-heartedly, "We should hope to spend this summer not so much with each other as with ourselves. I am not your dearest of friends, nor is anyone else. You are. Each of us, more often than we think, need to lose distractions, including others. With any luck this trip will prove to be a wonderful opportunity to get to know yourself a little better. Spend your time. Be very much liberal and uneconomical with it."

I nodded with understanding, already and often catching myself lost within the long and silent seafaring moments. I also sensed how I was slowly becoming a quiet observer of thought and the world, but then countered, half-seriously, "What if I don't feel like knowing anything more about me?"

Plato laughed, then replied, "How unfortunate it is that most are scared to death of this idea and are incapable of even a modest attempt at it. Perhaps they fear who they will discover. Don't be afraid Paul. *Sapere aude.*"

We had uneventfully skipped down the better half of the eastern coast line of South America, spending little more than half a day in the handful of busy ports along the way; just long enough to unload bicycles and bring aboard something else. We never had enough time off the ship to get a real idea of the land and its people until we reached Rio de Janeiro. Ol' Cap said we were quite ahead of schedule and thought that we'd anchor offshore for approximately two weeks, if not more. We later found out that his wife and children lived here and like any good husband and father, Ol' Cap was in no rush to leave the ones he loved.

Our first evening out in the city was fantastic. Plato and I walked around for some time about the inner part of it then meandered back out to its ocean edge and, after poking our heads into a couple of places, we finally settled into a small but crowded bar that sat directly on Ipanema beach. We were lead by a magnificently cute little waitress to a small cafe table at the corner of a packed dance floor. Live music was being played just on the other side of this dense and stifling room, and it was loud and wonderful. We couldn't quite see the band that was performing, but someone in it was hurricaning into a harmonica with uncompromising talent.

Both Plato and I leaned back into our chairs almost simultaneously, taking in our environment with broad smiles. The people dancing were in their own worlds of diverting employment, beautifully did they move, beautiful as they were. The body heat expelled from all of us in the bar would have been overwhelming if it had not been for the gentle sea breeze that kindly crossed the room, barely saving us from suffocation.

"I've never seen such attractive people," I admitted to Plato, yelling at him only inches from his ear.

"And whoever is playing that harmonica," responded Plato with a confirming smile, "has the gift of the Gods. I daresay he puts Beethoven and Shakespeare and Michelangelo to shame in their respective fields."

As our adorable waitress returned with some drinks, I observed Plato out of the corner of my eye. He scanned the room thoughtfully with a look of familiar contentment. It was as though he were recognizing people and objects he once knew from the past. As silly as it sounds, it appeared to me that Plato had always existed; as if he *never not was.* I realized then that he acquired the ability to anticipate life without panic or premeditation; as if he had been through it before, had even somehow been to this bar before. I suspected, if allowed, Plato would see it again somehow in some other time; to which I silently concluded, would not be a surprise to me.

"To top it off," Plato said, after taking a long sip from his drink, "our waitress is as cute as a button."

We didn't have long to enjoy the moment for we were dragged by terribly gorgeous women to the dance floor before we were able to take a second sip from our drinks, or, to tell them no. As we found out directly, it appeared that the female form was the true aggressor in this part of the world. I was easily influenced by one girl, but it took three or maybe four girls to convince Plato. Nonetheless, we both soon found ourselves in the middle of the floor packed like bees in a hive. I must fully admit that the women there dancing with us, and almost all over Rio for that matter, were nearly flawless in every way. They held the most exotic beauty without the slightest effort; and it was almost like seeing Emily around every corner and everywhere I looked. But, I daresay, the women here were almost more attractive and seductive. Almost.

Saved by the band taking a few minutes break, Plato and I crawled back to our table in sweat and exhaustion. It was at this point during our first night in Rio that we met Squatty. He appeared in front of us out of nowhere, and I nearly jumped in fright at the site of him. Although his appearance was indeed peculiar, I was more astonished that he was whiter than I was, which made a total of three of us in perhaps a ten mile radius. But he was so vastly white, so full-mooned pale, even in the shadows of this dimly lit bar, one would not be surprised if he had been born and left in darkness his entire life and only this morning let out to daylight.

From top to bottom there was no particular style he adhered to. Nor was there any favored direction to his blustering red and wavy thick hair, for it shot out from his scalp toward all points of the compass, defying space and time, like he slept on his head every night; upside down in a vacuum that was right side up. And although hair has no emotion of its own, Squatty's looked, at any angle, incredibly angry.

His skin almost looked more wrathful than the mop on his head, with freckles so tightly packed upon one another that they were almost impossible to decipher, and although taller in stature than most, he was nothing but skin and bones, except for his protruding white belly that poked out from the bottom of his too small of a sized tank top. It looked like he swallowed a basketball, or was similar in appearance of being six months pregnant.

After he thought Plato and I were quite done looking him over, he smiled warmly at us, with a smile that only worked on one side of his mouth, and said in a soft and almost feminine voice, "Is this seat taken?"

"Not at all," responded Plato, and kindly gestured him to sit.

Our cute as a button waitress almost immediately arrived with a green colored drink and placed it in front of our guest. He took a quick sip of it from the side of his mouth that only smiled, eyeing us both with casual glances.

"As you could imagine," he said finally, in his tiny voice, "I introduce myself to you both because we are of the same color and are rare sport in this part of the world, although the Europeans are catching on to this place rather too quickly as of late. My name is Squatty."

His matronly and *American* voice resonated through my head like a flute playing off in the distance, sweet and soft and almost insecure. Strangely, I wanted to hear more of it and noticed Plato being drawn into it too. As we introduced ourselves, he repeated our names slowly and soundly as we shook his hand. *"Plato." "Paul."*

As Plato caught him up to speed with our travels and existence there in Rio, I observed how some of the girls that walked by Squatty would gently touch him on his back or shoulders as they passed. One even slowed down long enough to run her fingers gently through his red violent locks and then gracefully continued on her merry way without saying a word. All of these beautiful girls wore big smiles of interest as they did, as if Squatty was some sort of toy, or hero rather, or even God. Squatty hardly seemed to notice as each girl placed their perfect little hands on him, and only seemed interested in what Plato and I were saying.

Our waitress arrived with another round of drinks without even being asked to, as all good waitresses should. Since I hardly put a dent in my first one, I politely refused the drink she placed in front of me with the wave of my hand. Her confused and pouty little face at the sight of my gesture nearly broke my heart and I was only saved by Squatty who witnessed the interaction and, as he gently held the waitresses wrist, said to her with a slight bow of his head, "Muito obrigado, Princesa."

"It is very polite around here to accept anything that is offered you," smiled Squatty to me, as our Button skipped off, coquettishly looking back at us as she did.

"In some ways it's hard to remember we are in another country," contributed Plato, "I keep forgetting there is no need to look over our shoulders. Alcohol is legal here."

Squatty laughed like the mating call of a coyote.

"By God," he said, "They *still* have Prohibition up there?"

"Yup, up there in the land of the free," I replied.

Squatty shook his head with a giggle, and shrugged his shoulders at the silly idea of it.

"One can easily trick boys with toys," he said almost rolling his eyes, and then quickly focused them, "But men are easier fools by rules."

Plato seemed to be as impressed by the words Squatty was saying as much as I was. We both were realizing that we were in the company of someone with as much depth in character as appearance, and even though this beautiful city of

South America had overloaded our senses in every way, we both felt like we needed to know more of Squatty, no matter where we were on the map.

Our conversation was interrupted by a deep voice across the bar.

"Squatty!" it called out.

"Oph, that's me. I gotta go," blushed Squatty as he rose from his chair.

He began to walk off, but then caught himself and returned to us.

"I play in the band," he confessed, almost apologizing, "It's fun. As someone said once, music is essentially useless, as is life, but both lend utility to their condition."

Plato and I exchanged quizzical and playful expressions at each other as Squatty shyly squirreled off to the other side of the room in his awkward and uncoordinated way. Within moments the bar quieted down as the dance floor once again began to fill up with shapely and energetic natives. After a few moments of absolute stillness, soft chanting began, and although I can't speak for Plato, I couldn't believe what my ears were telling me.

"*Squatty...Squatty...Squatty....*" whispered the crowd, slowing raising their volume.

"*What the....*" I heard myself say.

"*Squatty...Squatty...Squatty...!*"

Both Plato and I stood up, and since we couldn't see much past the dance floor, we climbed up on our chairs for a bird's eye view. Past the sweat and heat induced fog, and a few hands that waved high above heads to the chanting pulse on the dance floor, leaned Squatty against the opposite wall, almost bashfully, with a harmonica in his mouth. He slowly raised both hands to the harmonica and held it firmly. Then, even more slowly, he took in a long and deep breath. The crowd instantly dropped their hands by their sides and went silent.

Almost since the first day I met Plato, he often brought books for me to read, most of them being on poetry. Initially, I had a difficult time with the flow of the words and their arrangement, as well as their underlying meaning, but with Plato's patient encouragement, I slowly came around to the fantastic sentences that were formed by these wonderful poets from the centuries past and soon their words became poetry to my eyes, and my eyes became clear. When Squatty began to play his harmonica though, it was the first time I actually *heard* poetry, and it instantly enriched my ears, my mind, my soul, and my standard of life.

As Squatty moved his body to the sugar notes of his harmonica, I felt my mouth stand wide open in disbelief. Plato was motionless, almost hypnotized. Squatty moved like a serpent, low and smooth, in stark contrast to the physically awkward boy we had just met, as if he were almost more intoxicated by the music he produced than we were.

At this point, the rest of the band sounded in, and the dance floor ignited in energy. A few moments passed and I came to, looking back at the chair I was standing on, having no memory how I got to the dance floor, with Plato there, too, by my side, smiling, laughing, both of us surrounded by a sorority of dancing women.

Well into the next morning as the bar finally closed and we stepped out onto the warm sand of Ipanema, the sun was just starting to dry itself off from the ocean and the city was slowly rising from its slumber. Alluding to my thoughts of Plato earlier in the evening, I said to him, "If I only had last night, I think I could live this life over and over."

"Ehh," replied Plato with a smile but little interest, "To do that would be dreadful. The unknown is so necessary and appropriate."

I was a little surprised with his comment, for I had witnessed him throughout the night having as much fun as I. But since Plato *was* Plato, I consented to his intuition without responding.

"Alas," he then said with a chuckle, "to die a few times though, I have to admit, would be interesting."

With our shoes in hand, we approached the temperate water and let it decant our souls as the sun completely abandoned the Atlantic, making them both appear lonely and forlorn. The sun then quietly demanded our silence, which it was given, and in return slowly bestowed the nostalgic hopes and senses of my yesterday, reminding me of silly childhood dreams of my cornered youth that never materialized, but that I still hold close and dear to this day.

~

We crawled back onto our ship and slept most of the day away. Before leaving the bar, Squatty had said goodbye to us and asked us to stop by his place whenever we awoke later in the day. We were both excited to hear this since Plato and I were so instantly interested in him.

The sun was almost setting again when we knocked on Squatty's door that evening. He seemed as eager to see us as a dog would be when his owner came home from a long day of work, and as so, invited us in as if we were family. His two room flat appeared more like a woodshed to me and not nearly as tidy or clean, but Squatty was as proud as a peacock of it, which instantly made the little dwelling a warm and welcoming home.

He graciously sat us down on wooden boxes and brought us wooden cups of warm and slightly grey water from the other room. He assured us the water was perfectly drinkable and gulped down his cup as if to prove it to us. He then said, after wiping his mouth and sitting down on the floor in front of us, "I'm so glad you're here. For some reason when I first saw you guys I knew I had to get to know you better and not just because you were white, or American."

"But how did you know we were American?" I asked.

"Believe me," Squatty laughed, "You can tell us Americans from a mile away. We stick out like sore thumbs."

We all shared in a brief chuckle with the acknowledgement that somehow this was true. Plato then chimed in, "How long have you been down this way?"

"Oh, just over a year now I suppose," he said, counting his fingers as months.

"Any plans of returning?" I interjected.

"Not for a while, I guess, if ever. I left Oklahoma not because I wanted to. But now that I'm here, I couldn't imagine myself anywhere else."

"I see," observed Plato, sensing the slight tension in Squatty's voice, "And is Oklahoma the place where you became proficient with the harmonica?"

Squatty laughed. "God no," he said, "I only learned how to play a few months ago. I found one on the beach here and just started blowing through it."

From what we heard the night before, I had a hard time believing Squatty, but Plato appeared content with his answer.

"I guess I have love to blame for playing the way I do," continued Squatty without being prompted, "The first note I played through that sand-infested harmonica reminded me at once of the love of my life. Every note thereafter, I suppose, I have played for her."

"Wow," I said innocently, "Is she from around here?"

"She's dead," immediately replied Squatty with a quiver to his mouth, "She's the reason I left, the reason I'm here."

The room went quiet, and Squatty slumped his shoulders more than they already were very much slumped and, without restriction, and with instant tears over and down his tightly freckled cheeks, cried more than any cloud I have ever stood under.

"She hanged herself," he whimpered through his tears, "in my family's barn."

Plato and I continued to remain silent. There was nothing more the moment allowed. It was only when Squatty began to compose himself after some time, I gently put my hand on his shoulder and whispered, "I'm so very sorry."

Without looking at me he nodded, and then leaned his back against the wall behind him. He tilted his head and stared up at the ceiling, shifting the tracks of his tears as gravity transposed them from the front of his face to the sides of it.

"Why is it," he pleaded, "that I feel this way? Still? Why do I, being who I am, and knowing what I *believe*, cry on a moment's notice at the thought of her? I know for certain that I will be with her, when I am no more, and we will be back together then. Forever. What is a couple of years on this earth compared to an eternity? Why am I not pacified with these thoughts?"

Being questions that didn't require answers, the atmosphere was heavily muted again, and

Squatty threw his face into his hands, reigniting the sobbing he began with.

"Perhaps," said Plato in a soft and delicate tone, "it is not for anyone to know, but there is always sadness with truth. Death is universal *and* personal, and there may exist a small part in all of us that senses we will never see that person again, regardless of faith, regardless of belief. Death offers no interpretation to us, only we to it."

Squatty looked at Plato in desperation, like he was internally fighting with his mind and heart over reason and emotion, and then, giving up on both, stared at the floor in front of him.

"I'm just so insecure," admitted Squatty without emotion, "because of the love I have for her. I am helpless."

"We are all insecure," countered Plato, "No matter how confident some seem, they aren't. They simply know how to hide it better. For myself, I sit at the top of this long-listed and heavily flawed character trait."

Squatty cracked a small smile at Plato. He ran both hands through his red mane and then shook his head like a dog that had just came out of water.

"You may be the only one in this world who isn't insecure, Plato," replied Squatty.

My eyes relaxed a bit with this being said, observing how Squatty realized the person Plato was quicker than I had when I first met him.

"Alright, alright," Squatty said, changing gears, "Enough of this. Let's get out of here and do something."

I started to get up from my wooden box as Plato and Squatty began to leave the room. Squatty stopped in his tracks and turned to us both.

"I'm sorry for all that," he apologized, motioning to where he was sitting on the floor, "I'll try not to be so pathetic from here on out. No promises though."

Squatty half smiled again with a faint spark in his eyes.

"Say," he said, like an idea just entered his thoughts, "do you mind if my flatmate tags along?"

"Why not?" I said, as Plato agreed with me by gesture.

"Great!" Squatty said with excitement, and then looked down at my feet, "JUJU! JUJU wake up!"

Not six inches from where I sat, a movement was noticed under the small pile of dirty clothes and garbage that Squatty was apparently collecting in the center of the room. Like a jack-in-the-box, a small boy sprang up from underneath it in one quick movement, standing motionless with a bowed and obsequious head. So startled was I, that I nearly jumped out the only window of that woodshed. Squatty and Plato both burst out into laughter at my reaction.

"Don't worry," Squatty said with assurance as he continued to laugh, "he's perfectly harmless."

I looked JuJu over with fascination. His body was so perfectly miniature that I wondered if he weren't more china doll than human. From the neck down he was not quite the age of a toddler, but his head was covered in tight and dark gray curls that were thick as molasses. His more whitish-gray beard nearly reached his chest but I still couldn't tell, with all honestly, if he was 9 or 90 years of age. The very highest curl on his head didn't quite reach my elbow in his overall height, even on tip-toes, and he was not so black in color as he was brown, perhaps from years of the jungle becoming his shade from the tanning sun. With just a day or two lying out on Ipanema beach though, I was almost sure he would turn black as coal. What added to his mystique was that he stood as still and as quiet as a coffin, and if he hadn't been standing, or if I hadn't seen the slight rise and fall of his chest, I would have thought that he belonged in one too.

On the way out, JuJu donned a robe and grabbed his walking staff that had a long arcing hook at the top of it and that reached more than twice his height. To me he looked like he had just stepped out of a page from the Bible, resembling a shepherd in the times of Jesus. I couldn't help chuckle to myself at how much an odd couple Squatty and JuJu proved to be. So very odd in fact, in both appearance and manner, I was confident that not the greatest of imaginations could have made the pair up.

Plato and I initial thought JuJu talked very little, but soon discovered that he didn't at all. This was of little consequence, for the rest of us made up for him, and our wild adventure that second night out in Rio consisted of walking down along the shoreline and then back up it, exchanging histories and thoughts, with each of us thoroughly enjoying where we were and whom we were with.

"If you guys are looking for work," said Squatty at his doorstep as our evening was at an end, "I can get you some. It's hard going and not much money of course, but it almost pays the rent. If you're interested, meet me here at sunrise tomorrow."

By the time I got into my sleeping hammock I was more awake than I had been all day.

"I can't believe Squatty's girlfriend took her own life," I whispered to Plato, even though no one else was around.

"Perhaps she saw the reality of things," he responded, half asleep, but fully serious.

"I couldn't imagine killing myself because of it, though."

In the darkness of our little sleeping quarters, I heard Plato shift in his hammock to gain a better talking angle.

"Someone once thought that suicide was a philosophical problem," he said, "It's not. It quite possibly could be the only true enlightenment in its purest form."

"Whoa," I said after failing to wrap my brain around his words, "Do you mean I have to kill myself to be enlightened?"

"No," said Plato with a faint and underlying chuckle, "But once enlightenment is achieved, I suppose one may want to. Otherwise and for the most part, we are too self-absorbed and important and want to live forever. Or worse, we want to kill others instead and infinitely more often."

"Either way," I stated, "I hope I'm never enlightened."

"Don't worry," laughed Plato, "Most of the world isn't anyway."

"But to kill your *own self*," I persisted, "I can't possibly imagine it. Certainly nothing is worth that."

"The highest price paid in life is not death, Paul, for that is nullified by birth."

And before I could ask my next and obvious question, he answered it directly:

"No, by far and away the most unsurpassed toll of existence is possessing the awareness of time."

8

Plato and I couldn't guess what Squatty did for work, and for that main reason we decided to rise early and meet him the next day to find out. Regardless of his employment, I desperately needed the money, and up until that point in the trip I was able to skim by all on my own without Plato's assistance.

"I bet he cleans hotel rooms," I said to Plato, as we were walking to Squatty's flat just as that wonderful sun was piercing through the ocean again, casting infinite shadows on the earth while chasing its own at the same time.

"Nah, I bet he works at a bank or something, suit and tie and all," Plato said.

As it turned out, Plato and I were both wrong. Within an hour, the four of us(JuJu in tow), had one of the best views in the world, or at the very least the best view in Rio, for we were atop Corcovado looking down on the city of Rio de Janeiro and the Atlantic ocean just beyond. The world famous Christ the Redeemer statue that sits on the very top of this mountain was set to be unveiled to the world the next Fall of 1931, and even though it had several delays with its completion, by the looks of its current situation it had a lot more to do in order to make deadline in just over a year. Our boss, in his perfectly harsh and extremely loud Portuguese, continued to remind us of that almost every hour of every day for the nearly two weeks we shoveled and wheelbarrowed up there. The four of us worked hard and I daresay harder than anyone else, for it seemed the locals were somewhat allergic to their jobs. Perhaps they were clever enough to pace themselves, for never was there any hustle and bustle and stress among them, ultimately proving a wonderful way to exist.

"The only thing better for the mind than study and reflection is hard, physical labor of the body," said Squatty in his completely exhausted and feminine voice during lunch break on our very first day.

"Give me a book any day over this," I retorted, just as tired as he, "even a dictionary."

Squatty gave a short chuckle and then suddenly caught himself as if he were trying to stop a sneeze. An idea directly hit him in the face, as most of them appeared to do, and threw off the natural course of his humor.

"Say," he said, wiping his mouth with the back of his wrist, "There's supposed to be a full moon tonight. You guys want to sleep up here? The stars are so close sometimes that you could almost bump your head on one."

We all agreed unanimously with big smiles, except for JuJu, of course, who remained silent. After the sun had long set, I initially thought that we were stowaways again, sneaking onto a mountain this time instead of a ship, and as such, thought we would be the first and only pioneers to do so. As it turned out, a lot of our fellow laborers simply slept up there most nights of the week, leaving families and homes miles away below them, but saving time with their commute.

"Gosh," I confessed to Plato that evening as we watched our co-workers settle in for the night, "I really thought we'd be the only ones up here. I don't know why, but for some reason I was certain no one else had thought of this before."

Plato smiled in his usual way, slowly shaking his head, being well adjusted to all the silly questions and observations I had asked him since the day we first met. He turned to me and said, "*Nullumst iam dictum quod non dictum sit prius.*"

It wasn't until we got all the way back to New York City that I was able to translate what Plato said: "Nothing has yet been said that's not been said before."

The stars that night were indeed so clear and close, that if I hadn't been so afraid of fire and being singed, I would have thought I could have reached out and extinguished each one with my thumb and forefinger. The moon itself was never bigger, and lit up the mountainside like a spotlight, helping me to write in my journal and making us all feel like it was too early to go to sleep. Its pale hue color matched so perfectly with Squatty's skin that it made one wonder if there were not some sort of direct history between the two, as if he had been born there, or molded from its dusted clay.

The first time I heard JuJu's voice was that very same night. True to his native tongue and what Squatty said was his tribe's deep jungle custom from whence he came, each and every night JuJu sang himself to sleep.

Up on this highest lookout in Rio, he sounded like a melancholy instrument of the most contented sadness; like a lone oboe, soloing in a great and empty amphitheater. His music was filled with long, solitary notes that seemed to calm everything within its range, even the wind and the ocean beyond, like a halcyon, and I too fell under its spell with little resistance. The men who slept around us on the fresh dirt they shoveled just hours before, made no complaints of JuJu's lullaby and quietly snuggled into the earth like amphibians beginning their winter hibernation.

As with every night, I longed for Mary's company, but this time, whilst on the dark side of the earth even with the heated sea breeze warming me, the absence of her made me shudder for a moment and chilled me to my core. Yet at the same time I was alive and real, and transcendent, and although the gods would not approve, with one word from Mary, I would sever one of those stars for her in her honor and match the energy from this event with the love I had for her in my heart, even though it was severed as well.

I was awakened from my physically exhausted coma the next morning by the persistent nudge of Plato's elbow. The sun was taking center stage once again and showing off its physique with its early morning routine. As I sat up next to Plato, I noticed I was the last person to rise. My fellow co-workers that littered the mountainside, all sat facing the same direction as we, slowly adjusting to consciousness and the realities of non-slumber, and all having what looked like a staring contest with our closest star.

For nearly ten minutes no one made a sound or moved a muscle, and the scene reminded me of prairie dogs in the midwest of the United States, that upon hearing a threatening noise, would spin their heads in unison to its source with complete attention and focus, yet remain perfectly still.

"Funny," I heard Plato say out loud, but completely to himself and not to me.

"....Funny....how....?" questioned I after a moment, butting in on the conversation he was having with himself.

"Oh, nothing," he said with distance in his voice, "I was just thinking that we all seem to have the same view of the world from the same distance and angle, no matter how different we think we are as individuals. But I wonder, if we only took just a half step backward, would we realize how silly and preposterous most of our thoughts and actions were, and how desperately we need to change them?"

"Perhaps people need to travel more," I offered, with shallow confidence, "Maybe getting out of one's comfort zone is a good place to start."

"Travel is not necessary but boy, how it opens the mind," replied Plato, "It is true I have known some who for their entire lives did not leave a three mile radius from where they had been born, and were more worldly than some of the most ardent globetrotters. But the more you see of the world the more you see of yourself. It is an entirely selfish act, yet it appreciates the soul and how you see the souls in others, and ultimately instills knowledge of the vast capabilities of the human heart, for we all share the same and solemn rhythm."

No one needed to know our names there. Plato and I were anonymous, free and accepted. The same went for Squatty and JuJu too. Time was suspended, or rather, we stole it when it wasn't looking and stood it on its heels. Although we knew the world was still spinning, our existence was not. For me it was one of the only moments when time did not hold me hostage. It reminded me of a line I read in one of Plato's books, *"...when in eternal lines to time thou grow'est."* Whether Shakespeare knew the massive weight of this line I know not, but I felt as though I were caught up in its current there in Rio de Janeiro, and holding onto the end of it, if only for a moment or two.

But alas, Time eventually got the upper hand, as she is very much undefeated in this regard, and deceived us back double fold. I had such fun and rich experiences those quick and lengthy two weeks in Rio de Janeiro that in spite of my heart longing for home, the rest of me did not want to leave. When the evening came for us to board ship and say goodbye, there was a physical shock to my person that denied any departure.

Squatty didn't want us to ever go, and within the final hours of the ship pulling anchor and shoving off, we simply asked him if he wanted to come with us. He gave us a look as though the suggestion could never have been thought of in a million years. Then all at once he gave us that familiar half smile and said, "Well, why not?"

He immediately turned and ran off towards his flat, leaving JuJu standing alone and abandoned in front of us. JuJu, realizing his situation, silently turned towards the direction of his roommate without acknowledging us and followed suit, pedaling his little feet so quickly that his lower half looked like a blur. He caught up to Squatty in almost no time, following close and directly behind him with his staff held horizontally in the air above his shoulder like a javelin.

As we were saying our goodbyes to the ones we had grown close to at the beach bar where Squatty was legend, and which had wonderfully turned into a sub-family all of its own, I discovered Plato had slipped off and away without anyone seeming to notice. So, I too snuck off to look for him. He had not wandered far, as I found him sitting on the belly up side of a small skiff that was beached on the shoreline and straddling the impending tide. His familiar preoccupied countenance had settled in his face and he looked as though he were staring at something off in the horizon although nothing was there but sea and sky.

"Penny for your thoughts?" I asked, almost startling him.

"Oh, I was only just thinking of a new religion. That's all."

His comment startled me in turn, instantly spinning my emotions of self-absorbed importance to that of reserved and self-less thought. I never had imagined that a religion could be invented until that moment, and I never had met a person before or since that ever thought to make an attempt at one.

"I believe in it without knowing anything about it," I said to him with raw honesty.

Plato laughed.

"I think that is what they call f*aith*, young Paul," he replied.

The conversation was interrupted as our ship bellowed out a low and almost irritating tone from one of its horns. Departure was imminent.

"Well, you'll have to tell me all about it on board. Ol' Cap is pulling up anchor so we better censure our beliefs and make haste," I said in a fake indifference, attempting to cover my fear of missing the boat.

As Plato hopped off the skiff and walked pass me toward our little dingy to cart us out to the ship, I turned around quickly to follow, and as I did, nearly ran over our cute-as-a-button waitress from Squatty's bar who had served us that very first night in Rio and almost every night thereafter. She was standing there quietly behind me with tears in her irresistibly large and dark eyes. Instead of taking a step back, she took one forward and kissed me directly on the lips. She then took both of my hands in both of hers and held them as tightly as she could for several moments, carrying a look of bewildered and intense sadness on her face as though she would never see me again.

As it turned out she was right, because she never did.

"*Muito obrigado*," I whispered to her, "Thank you. For everything."

Squatty and JuJu had yet to arrive from their flat and I was beyond worried that they would not only miss the trip, but that Plato and I would also miss saying goodbye to them. Yet, out onto the beach came the two at full tilt, with Squatty carrying what looked like all of his possessions he had ever owned under his arms and on his back. JuJu followed directly behind him, carrying much more than Squatty, carrying more than his own weight in multiples, like ants or other insects are famously known to do.

Within only a few feet from the water, Squatty caught a small hill of sand with his foot and cartwheeled into a face plant that shook the earth. After our small farewell caravan on the beach rushed over and realized that he was okay, they, almost in unison, burst out into the most uncontrolled laughter Ipanema beach had ever heard. I even noticed one little boy had urinated in his own shorts from Squatty's hilarious acrobatic performance and so embarrassed himself that he dove directly into the ocean to erase the evidence.

When Squatty finally scraped off the majority of sand from his face, a dusky-coloured and smartly curved girl emerged from the group. She walked up to him and passionately kissed him on the mouth, wet and heavy, for what seemed like an uncomfortable eternity, then pushed him away and walked through the crowd and off the beach with a gait that carried a severely weighted heart.

"Geesh, what a knockout!" I exclaimed to Squatty in a whisper.

"Eh, she kisses like a cow," he demurred.

"Have you really kissed a cow before?" piped in Plato.

"On a bet, yes."

We hugged everyone goodbye again and again and shoved off the beach waving with arms high all the while. I was mostly drawn to the cute-as-a-button waitress waving to us desperately with those same dark and teary eyes. Plato caught sight of her, too.

"There is nothing more a heart can miss," remarked Plato, "than a soft and sweet forbidden kiss."

I said nothing but smiled and shook my head. The moment reminded me of an earlier statement Plato made back in New York when he caught me staring at a girl across Washington Square Park: *Beauty mocks an honest man for being honest.* I then realized with moral astonishment that I had kissed three girls inside of a year, and I don't pretend for a moment that I am some Casanova, but I felt almost ashamed at my behavior. Little did I know at the time that those three girls, Mary, Emily, and Button, would be the only girls I would kiss in my fantastically short career as a philanderer.

Just before we left Rio, I, of course, mailed a letter back home to Mary, even though she was almost as far away from Charlestown as I was:

Mary,

Come, let us make life deathless,
you and I.
Hand in hand, heart with heart,
run and jump,
Must we try.

Paul

~

When I was making room for Squatty and JuJu in our small sleeping quarters below deck, I moved my large duffel bag and discovered I had completely forgotten about the football I had packed for the trip before we left New York. I was almost concerned with how little I thought about the game now, compared to how much it consumed my thoughts and actions for most of my life, and how very much it was quickly becoming a fond and equally distant memory to me.

But when I brought the football up on deck to the rest of our gang lounging on crates, Squatty's eyes nearly popped out of his head when he laid them upon it, and immediately jumped up and ran towards the bow of the ship.

"I'm going long!" he yelled, "Throw it! This is the game winner!"

I gave Plato a subtle and smiling shrug and then launched the football high up into the air. With every bit of his awkwardness, Squatty, who managed to get some distance between himself and the rest of us on the nearly football field-sized deck, was now twisting and turning and stumbling over himself to get situated under the falling prize in order to win the game he thought he was playing.

At last he finally planted his feet in position and outstretched his arms to the sky. The football went right through his hands and smacked him directly on his forehead, ricocheting off him at an angle and sending the poor ball overboard and into the sea.

"Well," laughed Plato, "That ended quicker than it started."

As if hearing an alarm clock go off in his head, JuJu stood straight up from his crate, laid his staff on the deck, and jumped head first over the railing like an Olympic diver and into the ocean more than 20 feet below, hardly making a splash. In no time he tracked down the football and held it up for us to see, and although little JuJu swam like a dolphin, he was no match for the ship that was now up to speed. We soon realized that he was losing ground on it. Thank God for Plato's quick thinking, for he found some rope on the other side of the ship and after tying one end to the railing, he threw the other toward JuJu far below and away. By the luck of JuJu's little beard he caught the very last inch of that rope with the very ends of his little fingers.

It was nearly an hour before Squatty, restless on his crate, succumbed to his emotions and stood up proclaiming, "I know I can win the game, throw it to me one more time! Please! As God is my witness, I know I will catch it!"

If the event could have been captured on film, the audience would have thought the projector had skipped, reversed, and played the exact several frames over, for the *exact* thing happened as if we practiced the routine for months. The poor football slipped through Squatty's hands, hit his forehead square and sound, and over the railing it fell into the ocean once more. So identical it was to the first time, and so true to a performance that Squatty repeated, we wondered which one really happened and if time travel was actually possible.

Only this time, when JuJu sprung up from his crate to save the day once again, Plato was there with a firm hand on his shoulder, shaking his head to JuJu, whispering softly, “No, not this time, my friend. Let’s let this one go.”

When Squatty staggered back to us, rubbing his head in pain and astonishment, he uttered the only words the moment could allow: “I’m sorry,” he whimpered.

I stared with inclination at Squatty as he rubbed his forehead with a squinting, painful look on his face. In an odd way, he reminded me of a beautiful poem. He was the type of poem that didn’t rhyme though, and as wonderfully written as he was, he did not have the flow and rhythm of a rhyming poem. He was a *blank verse*, much too awkward and inconsistent to keep a repeating tempo. I couldn’t have cared less about the silly old football that had been thrown out last season anyway, but it weighed on Squatty tremendously. Whether he was born with having difficulty excepting loss or he acquired it through experience, I knew not, but in either case there was something very sententious about him.

“When it comes to life, I’ve never really won,” he said, not really addressing anyone.

He paused to think.

“And I’ve never really lost, either. I’ve always just been in this mediocre gray area.”

And then he thought some more.

"So that pretty much means I lost," he chuckled, starting to get over himself.

"Don't worry," I added, "No one wins in life anyway."

"No one has to," said Plato, ending the conversation.

It was only our third night away from Rio when I discovered that we had another stowaway aboard ship. I heard a faint and unfamiliar giggle from close by as we slept on deck and under the stars those first few nights out at sea. As I knew Squatty and JuJu were on the crate to my right, the muffled giggles were coming from my left and on the exact crate Plato was slumbering.

I remained low and quiet with wide eyes toward his direction and couldn't make out much from the cover of night until I saw an object break the shadows of the ship and become exposed by the chalky starlight. Just as I made out the silhouette of a girl with long wavy hair, she jumped down from Plato's crate and ran across the ship to a door that went below deck. Mind you, Reader, it is worth noting that this was performed without a sound by the impossibly pretty girl and, quite naturally, without a stitch on her person.

"You're experiencing a very lucid dream, Paul," whispered Plato, sensing my shocked consciousness, "In a *non compos mentis,* whatever you do, don't wake up."

"How did you sneak this one on at Rio, Plato, with all those there to see us off?" I whispered back, not missing a beat.

"I'm afraid she's been on board since New York," Plato admitted reluctantly.

"I thought all women were forbidden on any ship, especially this one?" I countered, remembering the lecture Ol' Cap gave us upon first boarding.

"I suppose you thought wrong," he replied in a tone that meant there was nothing to be said anymore, but followed not long after with a long sigh and said, "Sometimes I'm embarrassed that I am mortal. I feel more weak and ignorant than I already am. I feel selfish. Yet, conversely, I become even more ashamed when I realize that if Father Time looked the other way from me and I were able to live forever, how much more time and fortune I would still devote, nay, more like *exhaust*, on the same things, especially anything to do with the female form. Hindsight is such an unpopular reality, but whenever I look back on life, I always wish I had spent more time with myself."

It was an exclusive moment where I observed Plato having real and raw regret. He knew he wasn't perfect and knew he never would be. This flaw, however, was within his capabilities to improve upon where other things were not. Yet, still he continued to fail himself.

"Plato, don't think for a second you're just like the rest of us, even when it comes to women," I stated, reprimanding and defending him at the same time.

"Of course then I become guilt-ridden to live," he continued, as if not hearing me.

"Yes. Guilt-ridden *and* insecure," I mocked, "That's exactly how I describe you to others."

"It's just.." said Plato with thinking hesitation, "every so often I am reminded how confined I am within this human skin, and as much a comfort it proves to be, it is equally a prison of inadequacy. Sort of like this ship and the ocean it sits upon."

"If you are tired of this ship, Plato, I'm sure Ol' Cap will kick you off without slowing it down if he ever finds out about that pretty girl that just ran below deck," I replied with a laugh.

"Ol' Cap is the only other person besides us who knows she's aboard," revealed Plato.

"What do you mean?" I blurted.

"She's his daughter."

I don't know if Squatty overheard or witnessed anything that took place that night with the newly discovered stowaway, but the following morning he looked like he hadn't slept a wink. As we all stretched our bones and got ready for the chores of the day, I watched as Squatty walked over to the side railing of the ship, leaned on it with both elbows and stared off into the sea without any sign of enthusiasm. I meandered over to him, as he carried a stance like he was shouldering the sky, and noticed his swollen and strained eyes directly.

"This earth," motioned Squatty with his chin toward the horizon, "with all the wonderful things it has to offer, and as perfect as it may seem, in the end, is nothing but a mass grave."

"That's the saddest thing I have ever heard, Squatty," I said with a depressive shock in my tone.

"Unfortunately, it's true."

Plato had quietly walked up behind us and was standing there a moment without anyone noticing. I caught him out of the corner of my eye and said, "Well, what do you think of that, Plato?"

Squatty turned toward him, leaning his back against the railing and supporting himself with his elbows again, but with his face now slightly lit up with the expectation of his answer.

"There is much dark matter in the mind," said he, "Not the evil or disheartening dark, but the kind that deceives the self and escapes the light. The kind that slowly erases the memory of time and the length of existence. It condenses centuries to mere seconds, and the span of human life down to a single flap of a hummingbird's wing, and I've yet to distinguish if it's an attribute or flaw. Either way, we are terribly hurt when we can't find meaning in our meaningful lives. There is no doubt that life is fugitive, but the thought of it isn't, and upon that distinction lies the sorrow."

There was a moment of silence, and then Squatty burst out into laughter.

"Must you end every single conversation so wonderfully, Plato?" he yelled, and then laughed some more. Plato and I soon joined in with him, erasing somewhat the horrible night he appeared to have had, and furthering the depth and wonderment that he, and I too, had of Plato.

We trickled further down the eastern coast of South America in no particular hurry, stopping at ports along the way again only as long as we had to. It wasn't until we reached Buenos Aires that we actually set a sound anchor, and although it had the glitter and sparkle of Rio de Janeiro, we were all far too biased to compare the two cities. Rio was our home away from home, and we always found ourselves comparing and honoring it at every place we stopped.

We only stayed there two nights, and regardless of whether the sun or moon hung in the sky, we made the most of it. We absorbed the city and the wonderful people we met within it as much as we could, promising sleep to ourselves only as soon as we shoved off from its shore. During our brief stay I found a moment to write Emily a letter, which I include below, and mailed it to her upon departure from this fantastic city of Argentina.

Dearest Brat,

This southern America is everything one could hope and imagine it to be: beautiful people and beautiful scenery. You would fit in down here quite naturally, Emily, for not one thing is acted upon without fun securely attached to it.

Paul

9

The ship made only one more stop before we had to say our goodbyes to the Atlantic waters. It wasn't long after Buenos Aires that we started spending more and more time below deck due to the dropping temperatures. Even without the addition of Squatty and JuJu, our cramped sleeping quarters were crowded, stuffy, and hot; and produced a strong odor that reminded me of the football locker room back at NYU. But now with the additional roommates, it was twice that. Nevertheless, we still had excellent conversations, almost solely because we had nothing better to do.

"Who do you suppose," said Squatty one night after we packed ourselves into our stifling sleeping closet, "are the most unhappy people out there?"

The air was particularly heavy that night for we were into a bitter cold stretch of weather, and the entire ship was sealed up and sectioned off in airtight fashion, reminding me of what a submarine might feel like. It was so cold, that allowing fresh air anywhere below deck was not permitted for fear of ruin and exposure, and so we chose the lesser of two evils by sweating to death rather than freezing to it. We all were laboring to breathe, let alone talk, and so Squatty's question went unanswered.

"I suppose all of us on this ship?" he added through a smile.

"I've never really thought about it," said Plato, at a pace that mirrored the air.

"I would think it would be the poor," I offered, as if the answer was so obvious.

"Far from," said Plato, "They are one of the happiest I've ever seen."

"Agreed!" confirmed Squatty, nodding with a look of first hand experience.

"Most think the wealthy would perhaps be the happiest, but they are not," continued Plato sensing my desire for explanation, "Those that can just afford the necessities of life are the happiest, but don't realize it. The poor are universally thought they shouldn't be happy, but often live as though they were. But to answer your question directly, Squatty, I suppose the most unhappy people are those that continue to want what isn't needed."

Squatty and I didn't question Plato's answer, probably because we couldn't come up with a better one. So, our silence soon transformed to sleep, and words were not heard until the following morning when Plato, as was his habit, nudged me awake with his elbow.

"Hey, time to get up," he said to me in a low voice, "and don't tell anyone, because I'll deny I ever said it, but we may just lead the best existences in the world."

Being half awake, I only stared at him in complete shock and doubt of the idea, thinking of the endless amount of people who must be experiencing infinitely better lives than mine, even though I had little proof.

"The only rub, Paul," he added, sensing my thoughts "is that we keep thinking we don't and someone else does."

Ol' Cap began calling us his good luck charms. We made it around the bottom of the earth without incident. Never had he, nor any of his crew seen the waters in this region so calm and quiet, let alone during its current winter solstice. It was overheard one day by Squatty that some of the crew thought us wizards or demons of some sort that used secret sorcery to make the notoriously turbulent waters around Cape Horn as smooth as glass. When finally confronted by them, we confessed complete ignorance of the situation and that no magical spells were used by us or even could be, for we didn't have any at our disposal.

It did come as a humorous thought that Plato might later admit to me that he was friends with Poseidon and only cashed in on one of the favors owed to him. Naturally, I kept that notion to myself without giving up any chance of probability towards it.

And as for Ol' Cap's daughter, I never saw or heard of her again for the rest of the time aboard, even when we emptied the ship's pockets out in California. There was absolutely no hint or sign of her. Whether Plato simply rendezvoused somewhere else with her I never noticed or asked, but since he didn't care to mention her, then neither did I. Later on that year when we were reminiscing about the trip one day, I asked Plato how he discovered her. He confessed he honestly didn't know.

"I guess I just sensed her."

And that was all he could come up with for an answer.

~

We were turned North and well on our way up the side of the world when I realized the ocean had become a part of me, or rather, I of it. It was something I only felt but had difficulty explaining. I could identify with those sailors who hated the land and how they felt almost uncomfortable when near it. The change was barely noticeable, but there was an intimacy I developed with the water, like a gentle pulse to my soul that I had never experienced on any other surface or for that matter, with any other *thing*. It seemed to be acquired rather quickly, as I understood it sometimes could. Even though we were less than three months at the mercy of the ocean's fluctuating mood, I was seasoned and in tune with the affair we shared, and have yet to lose the quiet and timorous relationship I have with her.

One curtained evening, after the sun had just set and a silvered wind had dissolved as the waves fell silent and soft, the sea became uncharacteristically exposed; almost as though she were skinny dipping within herself. She appeared *see-through*, as if large spotlights had been placed on the ocean's floor and pointed upwards at the ship. I leaned unconsciously over the railing like I was about to hear a sacred secret of the universe. The moment was very much short lived, for her skin flushed all at once like a girl who got caught staring at a boy. Perhaps, she somehow saw her own reflection off the rising moon, or the side of the ship; or perhaps only noticed that Plato and I had been watching her intently and, up until that moment, anonymously. I, too, felt my face flush warm in reciprocation, for the event became almost undesirable, as if some form of innocence were lost.

"*Finis rerum*," whispered Plato to the ocean, with words that registered above my thoughts and intellect.

"How did the sea just do that?" I asked, as the embarrassed waters blushed around the ship and dissipated.

"I don't think it's the ocean," he said without taking his eyes from the sea, "It's what's in it."

As I returned my focus into the dark depths of the *incognita*, a large whale barely broke the water's surface, slowly and gracefully rolling itself, cresting and then twisting down from whence it came, just in time before colliding with the side of the ship as we passed. Both Plato and I instinctively braced ourselves for a collision but thankfully one never came. Before we could relax our stance, the ocean redressed herself in an instant and blanketed the event like it never took place, returning once again to her modest and discreet, lullaby cadence. And even though the sea is known to have no memory, she left Plato and I questioning ours.

"What unequivocal moments we are encountering on this trip," Plato said to me, with as much awe as I, too, was feeling.

"Thank you, Plato, for letting me tag along with you," I stated with earnestness after a few moments passed. "I'm indebted to you in so many infinite ways."

He only laughed in his usual way at me with a slight shake to his head. Then he playfully shoved me in the arm for saying such a silly thing that he thought nothing of, whereas I considered it an incalculable gift that enriched my life beyond both intellectual and spiritual measure.

Later, that same night, when we all had settled into our slumbering positions; JuJu sung himself to sleep, and Squatty quickly followed suit and fallen into his now well-known stuttering and lip smacking snores of ululation, I heard Plato, somewhat restlessly, turn in his hammock.

"Plato," I asked, before sleep acquired me, "do you think you're a philosopher?"

"God, no," he said in a laughing whisper, "I'm afraid I'm too happy to be one."

Before I could ponder my next question, it had already left my mouth.

"What is your mother like?"

"I knew her very little," he said seriously, opening up more at this point than he ever had to me, "But one of the last and one of the few memories I have of her stays with me. I don't remember what was said, or what she was doing at the time, but I remember the look on her face. It was a look of a very sad nostalgia. I felt like I could read her expression like a poem, perhaps because it was one, a beautiful one, and I understood her not as a mother, or a woman, but as a *being*. For only a short moment was this curtain drawn. It revealed to me this person who wasn't what I and everyone else thought she was, but someone who had been buried under the heavy layers of fabric and coats and make-up of life. It was well worn on her, for her precious face exposed to me her entire past. With one look, she told me that she fabricated her own fate early on hardly noticing it; because everyone else did the same as she; because that was how it was done. It was all that she knew and all that anyone knew around her. Without knowing any difference, she yearned for something more, or something else, even though she had everything that she dreamed of during her daydreaming days of youth. Indeed, all of her childhood dreams came true, but deep down she was unhappy, for reasons she couldn't explain, and wished she had dreamed of other dreams when she had had the chance."

"How old were you when you last saw her?" I asked, softer than a whisper.

"It was the same day I saw that look on her face. It was my 9th birthday."

~

Ol' Cap, for no other reason than the contentious fact that we were somehow behind schedule, began cracking the whip on the ship's engine as if we were being chased. Before we were to climb all the way up the continent and push off north from it, we had one last stop at a harbor in Ecuador called *Portuaria de Esmeraldas*.

Plato and JuJu skipped onto land to stock up on food from the busy market that sat right over the harbor's water, while Squatty and I stayed behind to help load and unload cargo. After a few quick hours had passed, there was no sign of Plato or JuJu, and Squatty and I feared they would miss the boat, for it was getting ready to depart.

As we were all for one and one for all, Squatty and I decided to jump ship and look for them, telling Ol' Cap of our plan before we left. He reminded us that the ship waited for no one, not even for his good luck charms, and we only had about an hour's time to find them.

We split up and raced through the crowded market as fast as we could, calling their names and frantically looking down side streets and under every canvas awning we passed. We both met back at our rendezvous in 15 minutes as planned, sweating and breathing heavily with no trace of them. Without having the slightest idea of what to do next, a little child tugged on my wrist. I looked down to see the most precious face in South America, with black frizzy hair that stood more than a foot high on her tiny head. She couldn't have been more than 7 years of age, and had only one word for me as she pointed inland just beyond the village.

"JuJu," she said, with a smile so innocent that I felt the entire world was free of sin.

"Yes!" both Squatty and I responded nodding, with eyes as big as saucers.

She led us through the market and down a narrow alley skipping merrily as she went, and before five minutes had passed, we were in a thickly settled forest, pushing away heavy vegetation on a footpath no wider than the deer trails I used to follow on the banks of the Connecticut River during the days of my youth. Ten minutes more and the path ended, dumping into a small native village packed with its inhabitants; and Plato, standing there at the trail's end waiting for us with a big smile.

"I know, I know," he said, noticing the desperation on our faces, "We have missed the boat. No worries, we'll catch the next one."

"But all of our stuff is still on the ship!" I said frantically, thinking of nothing else but my journal that laid abandoned on my sleeping hammock, "and we never said thanks or goodbye to Ol' Cap!"

"My harmonica!" realized Squatty all at once with a scream, as if it had just been stolen.

"I'm sorry," said Plato with sincerity, "I just couldn't say no to this place."

He slowly gestured with his arm around the village and as I followed it, I witnessed such joy and laughter among its residents. It was almost as if they were in the middle of one big celebration.

"How did you ever find this place?" I asked Plato, trying to understand him and our biggest mistake of the trip.

"JuJu showed me," he said simply.

"Where is he?" asked Squatty.

Plato scanned the village and I knew his eyes found him when the big smile he carried grew huge, nearly swallowing his face.

"There," he said, "By the fire, dancing."

With his walking staff pumping high above his head, JuJu danced around the fire like he had just found his Elysium. He reminded me of Harriet Smith and her unearthly state after she hit her famous home run. JuJu was glowing. I had never seen him so animated, and although he still carried his iconically flat affect, I could almost decipher a faint but bittersweet grin exposing itself now and then from behind that little beard of his.

"Is...he...showing emotion?" spoke Squatty, like he was witnessing a miracle.

Plato laughed.

"I think so," he said, "This village is his family, his people. He hasn't seen them in over 40 years."

Plato's intentions were slowly coming to surface. I think he enjoyed unfolding answers at his own leisure and delaying his reasoning to any topic as long as he could, for simple entertainment value if nothing else.

"Why did he ever leave?" I said, as I witnessed more joy in the last few moments of this village than I had seen in my entire life.

"It wasn't by choice," replied Plato, losing his smile, "Human poachers took him in the night and he became part of the slave trade before any one of his family awoke the next morning and realized he was missing. They inconsolably mourned his loss and thought only the worst for the past four decades, until this morning. At any rate, I thought the least we could do was support and celebrate with him, even if we do miss the boat."

And so we did, with everything we had in our hearts. There was so much love and laughter in this tiny little packed village that I thought it the sole generator that powered the universe.

"Well now," said Plato to me, as we sat ourselves on the ground to catch our breaths from dancing most of the afternoon, "What do you think?"

"I've never seen such happy people," I admitted.

"Nor I either," smiled Plato.

"And yet they don't have anything, or rather, almost nothing," I observed.

"JuJu's people may be the poorest people I have ever seen," added Plato, "not owning anything but what they wear, and what they wear is indeed almost nothing."

"But these people," I insisted, "Are the happiest people I've ever met. I can't imagine anyone more hopefully content."

"Do you remember, Paul, not too long ago, who you thought were the least happy people in the world?" said Plato, with slightly raised eyebrows as I acknowledged his reference, "Now do you see? It's no secret. This planet is past lease. *Possession is poison*."

~

We continued to celebrate through the evening and well into the morning hours, finally arranging ourselves on the ground by the fire to sleep with all of JuJu's people like sardines. Since bodies take up more real estate than their feet, every inch of ground was occupied, and someone stumbling upon this village may at first mistake it for a human lake or pond. Their unified singing soothed away any remaining care I had. With over two hundred people vibrating their vocal cords in soft and subtle tones, I felt more safe and warm and secure than a baby falling asleep on his mother's chest.

I didn't wake until the fire was completely out and the sun was well overhead. As I sat up, I observed Squatty and JuJu silently conversing by the trailhead that led back to the harbor, using only hand and head gestures. It appeared to be a passionate conversation, full of sound and fury, that finally ended with a sustained and heavy hug, and when Squatty made his way over to me, I noticed that he was crying.

"Is everything okay?" I whispered to him.

"Yes," said Squatty, "Everything is wonderful. JuJu wants to continue to be with me, with us, I mean, and continue on our journey. I'd hate to leave him, but I think he should stay here with his family."

"I agree with you," I replied.

"He told me that *I* am his family now," Squatty said, holding back his emotions as best he could, "And that no one matters more than I."

As soon as Squatty said this, I missed home and wanted to be there. For the entire trip I sent my parents a letter from almost every port, but here at Portuaria de Esmeraldas, I sent them a much longer one, thanking them for all the things they were to me and had done for me, and simply for being the selfless people that they were.

I gave Squatty a hug myself and patted him on his volcano-mopped head. Plato, smiling, appeared at the trail, and so I walked over to see what he was smiling about now.

"You're not gonna believe this," he laughed, "But Ol' Cap's ship is back in the harbor. Something about a broken propeller shaft. He told me that it was the last time he would leave his good luck charms behind."

I won't begin to describe the despair and disbelief after JuJu told his family he was leaving with us. There was an abundance of tears and long embraces, but he and Squatty promised to return as soon as they could. Plato and I encouraged them to stay, but both of them equally felt they couldn't leave us, and both knew that JuJu would never have found his family if we hadn't invited them in the first place. They strongly believed that they needed to see us through as far as they could, at the very least to California, if not all the way to New York. Perhaps, Squatty suggested, they could swing by JuJu's village on their journey back to Rio and stay a bit longer if the opportunity presented itself.

As the ship raised its anchor, I looked back at the small village to silently say goodbye. The sailboat masts in the harbor seemed to stretch to the sky in a forced haste; vying for position in an angular and angry tone, each longing for greater height and prominence than their neighbors but stunted all too soon by the capabilities of their makers and their own ancestral bloodlines. The inland mountains that rested behind the harbor were far more content and peaceful; satisfied with what they were and how high they had become and where and why they were placed. Countless millennia had not influenced any loss of serenity within them, only encouraged it, and I promised myself then, at the age of 20, that mountains were where I hoped to be when I grew older. They were where I wanted to be when I came to die. The restless sea was for the young, I thought, and the wise mountains were left waiting patiently for the old.

Our time on the ocean was soon coming to a close, for our next and last stop was Los Angeles Harbor. The unforgiving sea forgave in her indifferent manner and was ready to let me go. Being one of the lucky souls she did not choose to take, I in turn, was very much indebted though less willing to depart. Even so, I would soon realize I was ready for higher ground.

The last morning aboard ship I awoke early and dragged myself and my small blanket up on deck, wrapping the blanket around me more for company than warmth. I leaned against the railing in shadowed enchantment, looking west and attempting to discriminate the horizon that daylight had yet to disclose. It felt good to be the only one up. I felt good to be alone.

Before long the shy but steady illumination began to develop behind and over me, and the maternal sun allowed detailed access to me and those not borne for the night. As the gray curtain gracefully retracted, the distinction was revealed, but I blinked inconceivably at what I saw, as reasoning was defied; for there, spanning almost the entire rim of the horizon, sat directly on the spine of the sea a mountain range of immense size, likening itself to the Rockies of the Midwest, or the ominous Alps of Europe, yet so very much grander in scale.

At almost center stage of this production, and what stole the show altogether, were these silvery white wisps of clouds that rolled over the tallest peaks with incredible speed, vaporizing down in the mountainside, leaving no trace of themselves or their purpose. It was almost as though they were on their own horizontal axis, spinning over and down and then into the front of the mountains, only to pop out on the backside and repeat their somersaults over and again.

But this charcoal mountain range was not stagnant, for it grew and grew; and slowly rumbled closer and closer until it came towering over the ship; and did not become clouds until directly overhead. Even then I was yet convinced, until rain and thunder and lightening descended violently from them.

Standing there wet and alone, shivering from my damp blanket and the fear the storm had instilled in me, I would have believed anything was possible. I loved falling victim to one of Nature's tricks and beauty and power; and how she always, even as I stood there like a drowned rat, left me wanting more.

When I climbed below deck and found my friends still asleep, ignorant of the violence from above, like creatures in the ocean during a passing hurricane, I purposely clamored around loudly to wake them, for I wanted to share my fresh experience and tell them how easily and amazingly fooled I was by it all.

With poor translation of the enthusiasm I felt and perhaps mostly because they were still half asleep, the room did not seem as invested in my story as much as I had hoped for. I was losing ground with description, and trailed away from the story by drying myself off with a towel.

"Well, perhaps we all need to believe in something," I concluded, almost apologizing for my story and mankind.

There was no response until Plato slowly turned and sat himself up to physically wake his mental thoughts.

"It's not the fact that we are deceived in life," he said through a yawn, "but rather the colder and rarer realization that we desire to be; often craving it on a level higher than food or drink or sleep. Clouds are not the only impostors we long for. There are many other things that we let prey upon us; -but this, I'm ashamed to say, is one of the hardest facts in existence for me to accept."

"Would *love* be one of those things, Plato?" I suggested, like a fool who was knee-deep in it.

"Ha!" he laughed, and then raised both arms above him, "Love! Thy biggest and most sought-after deceiver of them all!"

"Love isn't the biggest one," said Squatty, rising from the dead in his hammock, "Life is the biggest deceiver of life. Things do not deceive us, we deceive ourselves."

Plato and I slowly and softly raised our eyebrows toward Squatty. He beamed with satisfaction at our expressions, and then his eyes became large and lidless, for a realization entered them.

"Well!" he said with more of a pulse, "How do you like that? I finally ended a conversation with something clever!"

As I changed out of my wet clothes, I quietly realized then that there is nothing more lonely and empty when a wonderful moment has realized its end, and sometimes, more often than not, words are not only overused and unnecessary, but experiences themselves do not always need to be shared.

10

We stepped off the ship for the last time thanking Ol' Cap and his excellent crew. Goodbyes are easily welcomed if one cares little about the people being left, but saying farewell to them caught me off guard. My emotions completely dominated my thoughts. It was almost like saying goodbye to my parents, knowing I would never see or speak to them again. I sensed that Ol' Cap and his crew felt nearly the same, as did the three others who left with me.

"For me," observed Squatty in a tone hinting toward the issues he had with loss, "this trip is a lot like life. Family and friends come in and out of it along the way, and memories of these wonderful individuals are glued to our wistful and sensitive conscious. What a bond 'Ol Cap and his crew will make on mine. What a magnificent bond!"

He looked like he was about to explode tears from every pore in his body, similar to when we first visited him at his flat in Rio, but this time managed to keep them back, or at least while in front of us, for he quickly turned and walked away toward the crowded seafront of Los Angeles.

Being back on our native soil felt comforting, for some odd and pride-ridden reason, and a strong sense of relief was hard to suppress in me. Yet, paradoxically, I had forgotten how insecure I was, and coming home made me realize how little there was of security within me. I somehow felt more afraid than I had been while far and away. Perhaps,

I was just homesick but was worried once again about being punctual. My main concern now was making it back to NYC for football practice. We had just over two weeks to travel from the Pacific Ocean to the Atlantic one. Nonetheless, there was a peculiar and unsettling sense about feeling unsafe that kept entering my mind after stepping off and away from the ocean.

Those vulnerable thoughts were not unfounded. Our first night in California was insulated with a fog so dense that it was difficult to distinguish our own hand at arm's length, and in turn further heightened our senses of our new surroundings. So, too, must it have forced the men and women in the city of Los Angeles indoors, or rather into every bar and speakeasy, so we thought, for the four of us were unable to squeeze into the first half dozen or so establishments we came upon.

The following night proved the weather played no part in public attendance, for these same places were just as packed as the evening before, only this time with crystal clear skies and near heat wave caliber temperatures. We concluded that the city was merely full of extremely thirsty and self-righteous people. Similar to New York, I was amazed to see the openness of alcohol and the consumption of it, for it seemed everyone had forgotten that we were still in the dry days of Prohibition. And just like parts of Manhattan, no one seemed to be aware of or remotely bothered by this national law. It appeared they couldn't have cared less about the silly rule, simply and most importantly because they didn't believe in it, as each and every one we met were all too eager to voice their unprompted opinions about it.

After finally wedging ourselves into a small and dark bar toward the city center, and being seated at an even smaller and darker table of an extremely dark corner, our drinks were ordered and nothing was said until our waitress returned with them. We let ourselves be too easily influenced by our surroundings.

"Well, the only thing truly immortal is death," toasted Squatty as he broke our silence and raised his glass in the air.

"To Death!" I joked, raising my glass to his.

"To Time," joined Plato, "The only thing I've found to be immortal, the only God I've ever known and feared."

Unfamiliar with the custom, JuJu sat still and only watched us, leaving his drink where it was placed by the waitress. I almost asked him to join in if only to clink glasses so he wouldn't feel left out, but remembered it was JuJu, and he no doubt thought us weird enough already and wanted no part of this strange seance. Besides, he couldn't reach high enough with his glass anyway.

"Whatever happened to the art of bowing when you greet a person?" questioned Squatty with a look of hard thinking after he gulped at his drink, "There's such a politeness to it. Somehow I think I must've lived in those times in some previous life, for I always have an inclination to bow when I meet someone."

"I fully agree," added Plato as he stood and then playfully yet gracefully bowed to us, "Propriety is lost without it."

Catching the silly moment, Squatty and I stood as well, and the three of us took turns bowing ceremoniously to each other for several moments. JuJu continued to sit motionless trying to mind his own thoughts and although he was born without facial expressions, he almost looked embarrassed for us, as others in the room began to take notice.

And so, too, could I tell, by that extra and instinctual sense, we were being watched without having to see with my own eyes. The ways of the world are always predictable. History proves as ignorant as the present and repeats itself over and over; and we, in the here and now, are always dumb and arrogant of our own superior intelligence. True reasoning is never constant and often forgotten within the challenged moment, and for the moment, within that moment, might is right and sins are born.

"Heh, heh!" said a man's voice perpendicularly deep as his mind was shallow, "Are you guys dancing with each other?"

The three of us stopped bowing and stood up straight, turning towards a very large and broad-shouldered man.

"And what about this tiny little thing?" he pointed, motioning toward JuJu, "Where did you find him? Under a rock?"

The big and hairy man grabbed JuJu's walking staff and looked it over.

"Hey!" screamed Squatty, "That's not yours!"

The man laughed again, only louder, at hearing Squatty's voice.

"I didn't know a woman was in our presence, fellas!" he said through his deep, rib-caged laugh, and then glanced back to his friends who were slowly gathering closer to our table.

Anyone who has ever been to a bar more than once, or a children's playground, could quickly and simply identify this lower form of human life. Their existence thrived on getting what they wanted through force. Reason never once polluted their simple minds, and as clever as Plato or anyone could be with conversation, there was no talking our way out of this one. The man's demeanor was direct, for he and his friends positioned themselves ready to take anything they wanted from us, only because they felt like it, and thought somehow they were entitled to any bounty just by being born.

"Give it back!" insisted Squatty, with an even higher voice.

"Oh, I'll give it back to him," said the brute, sizing poor JuJu up like he was a golf ball.

"Somebody save JuJu!" screamed Squatty as he dove under the table we were sitting at, curling up into a shivering ball with his head between his knees.

The man gave a short laugh at Squatty's bravery, returned his focus at JuJu, and cocked the walking staff back at full tilt as if to hit JuJu out of the crowded bar and back into the Pacific Ocean. JuJu only stood there in front of the man, in his usual still and dormant manner, and when the staff came swinging towards him at incredible velocity, he ducked down to the ground into a ball similar to Squatty, only with less shaking, and wrapped his little arms around his little bent legs as his staff whizzed by just inches above him.

Before the man had time to re-cock his weapon, JuJu rolled toward him as if to perform a somersault, but sprung himself into a forceful handstand halfway through it, launching his feet at the man's jaw and donkey-kicking his heels with precision and power at their intended target. The man's head exploded backwards, knocking him out cold before the back of him hit the floor, concussing everyone in the bar like a tsunami. The walking staff left the man's hand and JuJu caught it before it fell and then spun it around his tiny waist like some sort of Kung Fu Master. He allowed the rest of this posse, all six of them, to join in on the fun. Like a rabid squirrel in a tree, JuJu jumped and raced around them, pouncing on their heads and chests and shoulders, from one to the other and back with lightning speed, hooking some around the neck with his staff, or poking them in the eyes and throat with its opposite end, and before my mouth had time to open in disbelief, there were seven very large and near lifeless bodies on the floor. JuJu stood like a tiger above them, closely looking them over, almost begging to see movement so he could unleash more education on them.

The bar was then silent as a cemetery.

"Um...I think we should probably get going," said Plato slowly, breaking the eerie silence of the bar.

I grabbed Squatty from underneath the table and the four of us made our way out onto the street, tiptoeing silently away from the scene like it was a sleeping baby.

"Hey," said Squatty innocently, as we were trying to process what just happened, "We forgot to pay for our drinks! I'll be right back."

Before we could stop him, Squatty skipped back into the bar and within moments he returned, waving to us like there was no need to thank him.

"Don't worry, boys," he said smiling, "This one's on me."

Right on his heels was the leader of the pack, who somehow came back from the dead to the living, and as with any bully throughout history, the greater the bravado found on a man, the even greater insecurity is found within him. Since his pride was not yet as bruised as his jaw, he figured it hadn't quite enough punishment and urgently desired more. Squatty turned around to him and shrieked like an opera singer who just found out before intermission that his lover was dead.

The man darted to his left and towards his motorcycle that was parked just off the street and pulled out an iron rod from its sidecar. Before it could be put to use, JuJu silently pole vaulted himself with his staff over Squatty and came raining down on the man, all in one, fluid, mid-air motion, swinging his staff at the man's head like a golf club, almost in identical fashion to what the man had attempted to do to JuJu inside the bar just moments before. The poor bully fell like a sack of potatoes face first onto the street.

After the dust had settled and Squatty came out of the shivering ball he once again had positioned himself in, I went over to him to offer some support, for it looked like he desperately needed some.

"I thought you told me JuJu was perfectly harmless?" I said, with a bit of nervous and concerned energy.

"I...did," responded Squatty, more nervous and astonished than I was, "I guess you never really know anyone completely."

He then turned his attention to the bully who laid motionless by his feet. He bent over to his ear as if to tell him a secret.

"Next time," Squatty whispered with that half smile of his, "Try picking on someone your own size."

From start to finish the entire event took less than 3 minutes, including what happened inside the bar. Although I played no part in any of the action, I suddenly felt exhausted. I noticed Plato closely eyeing not the bully, but his motorcycle, as well as the other two that were parked next to it that just happened to be of the same make and model. I wondered what was going on inside his head.

As if reading my mind like he seemed to always and easily do, he said to me, "Do you know how to ride one of these things?"

"I do!" screamed Squatty in delight before I could answer, and he ran over to Plato to get a closer look, "Are you thinking what I'm thinking?"

After returning to our belongings that we had stashed at the docks the first day of our arrival, we rode directly east back through the city and were outside of its limits within the hour. The bully and his gang unknowingly loaned us excellent transportation. Fortunately for us, each of the three motorcycles had sidecars attached to them which served as perfect trunks for our gear. Although it was the first time I ever threw a leg over one of these motorized bicycles, after a few hours of bucking and rearing and stalling, I nearly got the hang of it.

We traveled through the night with our noses pointed east at a very slow pace, mostly because of my skill as a rider but also because of the subpar road conditions. We didn't seem to be too worried about what we left behind us, mostly because of what we had with us. With the aid of one or two street lights in each sleepy town our little caravan traversed through, I always glanced over to Squatty and JuJu with a smile, as the latter sat snuggly behind the former, clinging to him tightly with an utmost loyalty. The side of JuJu's face pressed firmly against Squatty's back, while one of his arms wrapped around his waist in a death grip fashion. His other arm held the tail end of his walking staff as the opposite end laid horizontally over the motorcycle's handlebars, protruding well over and beyond the front wheel.

Spearing the oncoming darkness, JuJu reminded me of a great medieval knight jousting his way out of California.

~

We finally stopped to rest for a couple of hours just before sunrise in a small town who's name I have since forgotten. After settling in behind an abandoned building and before JuJu began to sing us to sleep, Squatty pulled out his harmonica and played soft and sweet notes that complimented the oncoming daylight. It paired nicely with the silent and overtired mood we all shared and helped soften our bones and joints and muscles that became raw from the darkly intense and harsh motoring. Before I dozed off with my head against the rear tire of my borrowed motorcycle, I noticed a street sign out of the corner of my eye. Whether Plato realized it or not, he had stumbled us directly onto Route 66, which had just opened a couple of years previously. Not only did it head us in the direction we needed to go, it led us right through the middle of Squatty's home state of Oklahoma. I fell asleep with mixed emotions with the idea of this, for I feared Squatty was not remotely ready to return home. When or where Plato or Squatty realized this also, they didn't lead on, for neither of them said a word until we crossed its border.

I awoke a couple of hours later to Squatty and JuJu almost standing over me, having a silent conversation with their hands and heads again. It appeared to be another heated discussion and as soon as JuJu noticed me observing them, he turned and walked around the building that sheltered us from the road.

"What were you and JuJu just conversing about?" I asked, hoping to get a better answer than my obvious question.

"JuJu wanted to know what God was."

"What?"

Squatty sat down beside me and leaned his back against the motorcycle. He began to draw in the sand with a small rock he found beside him.

"JuJu has never found God because he didn't know to look for him," he said with reluctance.

By being abducted at such an early age, JuJu had been completely and miraculously sheltered from faith, and throughout his life by chance and circumstance, had not been influenced with any belief at all. He did not know the name Jesus, or God, or Allah, or any reference that was considered above a human or animal level. It's not that he didn't believe in any of it or had doubts about it; he simply had no idea the notion of religion existed.

We estimated that JuJu was close to fifty years old, which, as a side note, also had no effect on him in the least bit for he looked less than half that, as I've mentioned before, (perhaps too because no one remembered to tell him that we age and deteriorate as time passes). He made it through nearly five decades without being magnetized by any religion whatsoever and from what I could tell, lived a life of more goodness and selflessness than any religious person I have ever met or heard of.

"What he can't understand," added Squatty, "Is why heaven can't be here and now, and why we have to die first to ever see a glimpse of it."

"Sounds like fair reasoning to me," I said aloud, by mistake.

"What's worse," he said with a half smile, "When I try to describe God to him, he always points to Plato."

"So the secret's out," I laughed.

"If only he would except God into his life," replied Squatty with seriousness piling up in his tone, "He would see that his existence would be that much more fulfilling."

"It appears to me that JuJu has led a fulfilling life without God," I said aloud again, when I shouldn't have.

"But God made him!" pleaded Squatty, raising his voice in frustration.

"God created man," said Plato, walking up to us and butting in on our conversation with a smile, "And, to return the favor, man created God."

"Oh, that's not true," sneered Squatty as if someone else had said it, defending his beliefs over Plato's reasoning.

"Tell me then," pursued Plato politely but evenly, "Will JuJu ever make it into heaven? Even during the off-season? Even though he knows nothing of it?"

"I don't know, okay?" Squatty snapped back, torn between his beliefs and the horrific fact that JuJu may not be allowed past the pearly gates due only and exclusively to his status of pure ignorance of them.

At once the subject was dropped and since nothing else was left to say, we packed up and hit the road, riding as long and far as we could, catching a nap or a bite to eat when we needed to or when nature called for one of us, and talking very little, if at all. I could tell though, that all of us were thinking heavy thoughts. The wheels in our minds were spinning as fast as the wheels that carried us. As for me, I couldn't figure out which was more impressive when it came to JuJu. The fact that he had no concept of religion, or the miraculous ability he had as a warrior fighter.

After stopping to fuel up just after crossing the state line of Oklahoma, Squatty turned to Plato and me.

"I don't know if JuJu will make it into heaven," he said, like he was confessing his sins, "But I do know I won't be invited either if my mother ever finds out that I was driving through town and never stopped in to say hello."

The driveway to Squatty's home was literally attached to Route 66. If his mother had timed it correctly and had looked out her kitchen sink window while washing the dishes, she would have seen three motorcycles drive by her house had we not stopped.

As it just so happened, she was walking by her kitchen sink, and recognized her son immediately as we turned in. She came running out of the house and onto the front lawn like a swarm of bees was chasing her; flapping her arms wildly and screaming unrecognizable notes as they were staccato'd by her darting tongue that twisted and swerved out of her mouth like an anaconda. Her voice was heard clearly over the sounds of the motorcycles as she nearly tackled Squatty and JuJu off of theirs.

The only recognizable difference between Squatty and his mother was that she was shaped and shadowed like a cue ball. Every other physical molecule between the two was identical; even when it came to the hair on their heads. If both were actually wearing wigs, and they took theirs off and switched with each other, no one would know the difference. I somehow thought of the alphabet when I looked at the two of them embracing. Squatty was shaped like a lower case letter *b*, with his skinny frame and protruding potbelly, while his mother looked like an upper case *O*. Both shared the same and monovular font, yet Squatty's hue was a little more tarnished; or rather his freckles were more prominent, perhaps due from the year of a Brazilian sun. But so much were they alike in appearance and mannerisms, one would wonder upon first seeing them together if a father was ever invited into the offspring practice, for it seemed as if Squatty's mother merely cloned herself and became pregnant all on her very own.

After introductions, Squatty's mother, who insisted that we call her Suzi, graciously invited us into her home. As I was walking into it, I noticed the very large and somewhat leaning barn that sat off and to the right of the property. I was struck still at the sight of it, knowing it was the very place where Squatty's girlfriend had taken her own life. I was glad to be the last to enter their home, for if I had been the first, I would have stopped everyone from entering because of my knee jerk reaction to this barn. This would have further thinned this already fragile return of Squatty.

Suzi began cooking a large dinner as each of us took turns washing ourselves up. We all slowly migrated to the large oak-tabled dining room and before long, heaps of food began pouring out of the kitchen to land in front of us.

"Well, I've given it some thought," began Plato between mouthfuls, "I think we should decide when and how we send back our borrowed motorcycles that our friends in Los Angeles were kind enough to lend to us."

"Over my dead body!" grunted Squatty with a mouth full of food, "If they want their motorcycles back they can come find them, and if they find them, they'll get more of what they asked for when we meet up with them!"

"Mind your manners, Squatty!" piped in his mother, not so much concerned with the subject as its delivery, and slapped him on the back of his hand, "Don't speak through your food!"

Plato and I laughed unconsciously at their interaction.

"You talk as though you have an army of giants standing behind you," replied Plato, as he glanced over at little JuJu.

"Was it not you, Squatty," I added, "Who dove under the table at the slightest hint of confrontation?"

Squatty raised his eyebrows in acknowledgement and gave the food in his mouth a large swallow. He then glanced over to his mother and gave her a sarcastic yet playful look as if to ask permission to talk. She nodded even more sarcastically back at him.

"To be completely honest," he said, with undeterred confidence, "I've never been afraid to be a coward. In fact, I've yet to meet a braver man than I am when it comes to this."

We all laughed immediately and hard, and eventually so did Squatty, in spite of the fact he was trying to be serious. I looked over at JuJu and almost noticed a small crack of a smile, but as always, wasn't quite sure what he was hiding behind that beard of his.

"It's too bad the world over isn't composed of cowards," continued Squatty, still defending his actions, "For then we'd finally have a chance at peace on earth."

We all laughed again but more softly this time at the honest suggestion and thought of the possibility. I then quickly sensed that Plato was about to end the topic, as was his habit, with one of his thoughts, and felt a shiver of anticipation run up the back of my neck.

"One will always surely be wrapped by their skin," began Plato softly, "A loyal device it proves to be; so long as breath is exchanged in its owner. Yet anything outside of its boundaries matters little, whether threatened by skies or bugs, or oceans or bombs. It is on the bottom side of our cloaking where one finds its danger, its faults, its conflicts. And more often than not, our skin protects the *outside* from the *in*. Those that run off to fight in wars are the cowards. There will always be an endless supply of them, for they are far too scared to be heroes who fight the existing battles within."

With reflective thoughts of Plato's words and fatigue still very much weighing heavily on our shoulders, we excused ourselves from the evening of consciousness and thanked Squatty's mom for all her offerings. We retired early with the sun and our shadows. The darkness of the Oklahoma plains, as did our sleep, soon embalmed us anon.

~

Squatty slept that night in what seemed like a very deep and heavy sleep, for the rest of the house was up the next morning long before we saw any sign of him. As we sat down at the table for breakfast, I kindly asked his mother if I should go and wake him but she told me her poor boy needed the rest and he would come down to eat when he was ready.

"This almost could be considered a miracle with my boy's return," she whispered to me as I was helping her with the morning dishes after breakfast, "I never expected for him to step foot on this property again."

I nodded with understanding to her but said nothing. I could tell that her thoughts were concentrated and layered on this subject and consumed her mind even more so than it had her son. Spoken words, at least from me, needn't then apply; but when the big grandfather clock in the living room struck noon that day, I noticed even she was concerned about Squatty, and I witnessed her softly walk a few steps up the stairway to yell to him. With no answer after following up with a couple more calls, the rest of us started looking for him like he was a set of car keys. He still remained elusive and so our search soon spilled out of the house and onto the yard. We all had an unspoken feeling of where he might be, and when I noticed JuJu looking toward the direction of the barn, with his nostrils slightly flaring as if he had picked up

Squatty's scent, I immediately began to walk in that direction, hearing the others' footsteps behind me in obsequious pursuit.

It was here that we found Squatty lying on his side and sound asleep in the middle of the wide-pined wood floor, with a freshly picked bouquet of wild flowers resting closely in front of him. Upon closer look, he had tightly wrapped his arms around the flowers, like he was atop some precipice and holding onto them for dear life as if to save him; as if to be saved *by* them. The flowers were *something*, or, more conceivably, *someone* else.

The rest of us, including his mother, quietly circled and stood around him without making a sound. It was only after a few moments that he slowly began to stir. Squatty yawned and stretched and licked his chops without sensing us or his surroundings. With his eyes still closed, he sat up and folded his legs underneath him. A long stemmed white flower broke free from the bouquet as he did and managed to get caught up in his hair. It bowed over and down in front of his face like a tentacle, gently bouncing up and down on the tip of his nose.

Squatty, in his half-conscious state and with eyes still closed, began to swat at the flower like it was a mosquito, however the flower's stem was so well anchored into his thick mane that it kept returning to the tip of his nose like a homing pigeon. The harder he swatted at the flower, the louder our muffled giggles became, until finally he grabbed the flower with a clenching fist and threw it halfway across the barn floor. He then followed up with a '*hmph'* noise of satisfaction and a faint smile flashed across his face. Almost as quickly, the smile turned into a frown. He whimpered for a brief moment, coughed, then opened his eyes.

"Is it morning already?" he said to us full of wonderment and confusion.

"No, Darling," responded his mother, "We're actually in the afternoon now."

"Wow," pondered Squatty, as he wiped his mouth and began to rise.

He stood up slowly like an old man, like he had been sleeping on a cold and hard barn floor all night. I felt my face cringe because that's exactly what had just happened. I casually noticed the bales of hay that surrounded him, but he seemed not to be bothered with the idea of their comfort. It appeared, from where he laid, that he had actually pushed and swept them out of the way to make room for his unforgiving bed.

"Well," said Squatty breaking the silence after a few moments, "this is where I found her. Right here."

Squatty pointed to where he had been lying and carried an expression on his face like he was seeing her there now.

"It's funny," he admitted, with absolutely no sign of humor and a hint of irony, "I was born in this barn too."

I looked around as if to discover evidence of the very spot it occurred. The barn was as dark as it was dirty. Some twenty years ago, long before the refrigerator was invented, his imminently pregnant mother was fetching stored ice that was buried deep in the barn hay when Squatty decided he couldn't wait to come out. He took his first breath near a cow's udder, so his mother told him, and it proved to be the very same spot where his girlfriend took her own life, and conversely as well as very much symbolically to Squatty, took her last breath.

"I feel her very presence in this barn, like a heavy coat."

Almost unconsciously, he reached into his pants pocket and retrieved his harmonica, and then began to blow through one side as beautiful sounds came out the other. The bleeding heart notes each caused our own hearts to bleed and exposed the raw chords from Squatty's genius; the arctic and timeless music of unanswered love.

The swing of the large barn door broke our attention just as Squatty put away his harmonica. A small boy the size of JuJu poked his head around it as curious and as cautious as a cat.

"Hiya Sammy," said Squatty's mom, "Come on in. We're just having a little get-together."

The boy, who couldn't have been yet ten years of age, slowly tip-toed in as if he were testing thin ice on a winter's pond.

"Squatty?" he whispered in astonishment, after meticulously scanning his environment and its inhabitants.

"Hi Sam," chuckled Squatty with his half smile.

The boy relaxed his posture a bit and walked towards us, but then had a better and closer look at JuJu and returned to his defensive stance.

"I... I heard beautiful music..." said the boy, who couldn't pull his eyes off JuJu, which were just about level with his own.

"That's JuJu," said Squatty, "And this is Paul, and this is Plato. Everyone, this is our neighbor, Sam."

The boy quickly smiled and nodded at us but returned his focus back to JuJu.

"I... I've never heard such wonderful sounds before. I never knew my ears to be so happy, ...and...sad, too." continued the awestruck and contemplative Sam, and, after inching closer to JuJu and quizzically tilting his head at him, asked, "Did *you* make those sounds, JuJu?"

JuJu made no reaction of course, and kept his stare in front of him on the floor.

"No, Sam, I did." said Squatty as he pulled out the harmonica again. He pressed it to his lips and played, only this time with wild excitement and fervor, reminding me of the times back at the bar in Rio.

The boy had an expression like he had just been struck by lightning.

"By Golly!" screamed Sam in restrained disbelief after Squatty lowered the instrument from his mouth.

Squatty smiled and slowly held the harmonica up to the light so he himself could get an intimate look at it. He then looked over to Sam and then, ever so delicately, looked down at where he slept.

"This is called a harmonica," explained Squatty, "And I want you to have it."

The boy squirmed in delight as Plato and I exchanged thoughtful glances. He took the instrument from Squatty carefully with both hands and blew through it, unable to produce any sound but air.

"It'll take some practice," encouraged Squatty, as he patted Sam on the head, then sized him up, "Geesh, you're growing like a weed!"

Sam nodded and put the harmonica in the front pocket of his shirt.

"What did I tell you about poking your nose around this here barn, Sam!" screamed a voice from the doorway.

It was Sam's father, all big and burly and oozing with inebriation, instantly reminding me of the owners of the motorcycles we borrowed. The poor son ran to his father immediately with his tail between his legs.

"I'm sorry, Daddy," sounded the little cowering voice of Sam.

And then, with neither rhyme or reason, the horrific beating commenced, violently and swiftly from his father, with an open but heated and heavy hand to his son's head and neck and torso. Hard and convincing blows; making sounds that could shatter the thickest of human hearts within earshot; and again later and twice-fold upon reflection. Before any of us could blink the father then grabbed

Sam by the arm and yanked him out of our view, and we neither saw nor heard of them again.

"Well," said Squatty's mother in a defusing and uncomfortable tone, "his father *has* told him several times. I've heard him myself."

"That's *bullshit*, Mother," snarled Squatty, leaving little room for justification, misinterpretation and forgiveness. He then walked out of the barn without acknowledging anyone. JuJu followed him directly.

His mother stepped back in a bit of a shock from the language I never heard Squatty use before, nor from the looks of it had she. She said nothing yet, motioned as though she wanted to and ultimately compromised by casting a blank face toward the floor. After noticing that I was watching her, she gave an embarrassed smile at me and hurriedly walked out of the barn, following in the footsteps of her only child.

It was then that I noticed Plato. He was turned away from me, staring down as well, more still than JuJu, in his daily pastime, ever thought of being. His posture appeared to be stuck in a position he couldn't get out of.

"Are you okay, Plato?" I asked.

Plato didn't respond. He didn't even hear me. I wondered if he was experiencing some sort of seizure. It was as if his entire body fell into a catatonic state that locked him in where he stood. I half thought, with considerable doubt, that he was crying, perhaps from the violent event of child abuse that just occurred, but I couldn't quite tell from my point of view. I slowly walked up to him to get a closer look, and no, not even the slightest gloss could I detect from his eyes. He wasn't crying, or trying to hold back tears. He was *remembering*.

"Plato," I said, placing my hand on his shoulder.

He continued to keep still, and without moving anything but the muscles of his mouth, he said to me, "You are very fortunate to have a father like you do."

"I know I am," I whispered.

His stature relaxed only slightly.

"So... so stupid," signaled Plato slowly, and with almost no volume and much disgust, "What a waste."

Not knowing what to say, or rather what Plato needed to hear, I said almost arrogantly, "I *hate* ignorance. I hate it more than anything."

Plato came to upon hearing my words, and looked me straight in the eyes.

"No, Paul," he said firmly, "Those who hate ignorance or ignorant people, are ignorant themselves."

It took me just shy of two years to discover a crack or rather an exposed point in the nearly mythological-calibered armor worn by Plato. Perhaps he had allowed me to get a glimpse of it, but his Achilles' heel was revealed, if only for a split of a second. I felt as though I could see inside his soul long enough to confirm that he was not empty or indifferent, and that his source for such profound statements and observations since our first meeting did not go without some significant history and empirical weight behind them. Similar to the brief conversation we had about his mother aboard the cargo ship, he let me into his private world for a moment. Although he led his life *sotto voce*, it appeared to me he had lived an extremely long existence in his one and twenty years, and that he was still repairing a chink in his armor, a tear in his fabric. For an instant in that barn, I felt that all of his wonderful reflections and teachings did not just appear out of thin air for him like billboards signs on a drive around the outskirts of a city. No. I sensed they were somehow earned with great effort and perhaps great sacrifice, too. If anyone could mend a torn childhood, it would be Plato. But alas, there are things in life, despite infinite resources, determination, and ability, that have no cure.

~

Dinner that night started out very aphonic and perfunctory, with the only sounds in the silence being silverware hitting plates. But as the uncomfortable air got as thick as the pork chops we feasted upon, and almost as difficult to cut with my dinner knife, Squatty's mother began talking forcefully about the weather. When getting little participation from the rest of us, she then began talking politics.

"What this country needs is change," she said proudly as if she were the first and last person to ever say it, "and security too. Security."

"Moomm," moaned Squatty.

"It's as true as blue, my dear," she responded with absolute resolution.

"Suzi," smiled Plato after a short but adequate silence, "In my short life and little experience, I'm afraid I've found that there's no such thing as security. I believe there's an illusion of it for sure, that blankets this earth and those under it. But as much as you think that blanket gives you security, it doesn't. It is as transparent and as protective as the sky, and most wear it as if it were custom tailored for them alone. It's really nothing more than fabrication, mere smoke and mirrors. Be it someone killing you or you killing yourself, anyone, including me, can easily stop my life, but no one my death."

I noticed Squatty shift in his chair when Plato referred indirectly to suicide, but I also noticed that

Plato saw him as well, and somehow felt eased by it.

"As for change," he continued, maintaining his subtle smile, "Well, that requires less effort than to keep things the same. The real problems in this country are those who vote. If you want real change, don't vote."

Squatty's mother focused on her food with Plato's words, perhaps because she had no particular rebuttal. After no one else offered any additions to the conversation, Plato decided to politely continue.

"I'm always fascinated by the way things are," he said unpretentiously, "Civilizations balance on a blade of grass; yet so too does the soul of an individual. We are such fragile specimens, such brittle beasts. We do not always bend when a northwest wind chances by. No. We sometimes fold. And when such events occur, security goes missing without being missed, and suicidal tendencies hold hands with reality. It has been argued that this world couldn't possibly be the best of all possible worlds; that there is so much improvement to be made, so much imbalance to be balanced, so much more potential to be realized. But hope can travel you only so far before it reaches the destination of reality. Human nature conflicts with itself by these virtues. It seems as though the further one can stay away from reality, the better, for those who are depressed in life are not misinformed. They harbor too many truths, and the more truth one acquires of life, the harder it is to find it sustainable. Therefore, the only real security can be found in no other place but death."

We adjourned from the dinner table as the night once again threw her dark dress over us. I sensed our last evening, as well as our entire stay at Squatty's home, left us all slightly capricious and unsettled. There were many raw emotions revealed, and yet there was almost equally as much growth and understanding that was cultivated too. Indeed, much more healing would be required, including, and on a much more immediate yet insignificant level, my poor backside, for I did not wish to get on that unforgiving motorcycle upon waking first thing in the morning even if it was to save all of humanity. Alas, I realized all of these things would require time. Time, and the bittersweet awareness of it.

~

"It's too bad you couldn't stay just a few hours longer, perhaps even leave after lunch," said Squatty's mother regretfully to Plato at breakfast the next morning, "We have church. We all go to church in this town. Are you not worried about your life after death, Plato?"

"I'm afraid I'm not holding my breath, Suzi," responded Plato with a smile that already won the conversation, "But it is within our second nature to worry and, unfortunately, not until our seventh nature do we realize that it amounts to nothing. You calmly and confidently speak of eternity, but worry about the summer corn. Should it matter what the fall harvest yields each year? To worry, I think, is to be mortal. Right now though, I'm a little preoccupied with life before death. If I may ask antithetically, have you or your church ever contemplated life before life?"

Squatty's mother let her face contort into a look of fascinated confusion, like she never heard of such an idea. I too felt my face model similarly, for never had I heard of one either, but then thought of the religion Plato may have had in mind back on the beach in Rio.

"I doubt it, Plato," offered Squatty skeptically, "I do know that the reverend's sermons are regrettably *similar* to life though. They aren't horrible, but you find yourself waiting for something great to happen and nothing ever does."

"Squatty!" yelled his reprimanding mother.

As we started to pile up our motorcycles, I noticed Squatty and JuJu standing around aimlessly, and when they walked over to Plato and me, I said jokingly, "If I didn't know any better, it looks like you guys don't want to leave."

"That's because we aren't going to, Paul," whispered Squatty, barely able to look me in the eye.

Upon hearing his words, my mind was transported back on the deck of Ol' Cap's ship and I felt as though Squatty had swung its anchor around and hit me square in the chest.

"You can't possibly be serious!" I exclaimed desperately and in a knee-jerk way.

Squatty sighed. I could tell he was torn, but also very calm and very confident with his decision.

"I have a lot of things to clear up here, Paul. You know that as well as I do. I didn't expect to be back, ever, but now that I am, I've got to stay, at least for awhile, and see what I can get done and get through."

I looked at Plato for an answer, but his face was as composed as the one Squatty carried. He understood as did I, but it seemed as though he accepted it, as I did not.

"Okay, okay," I finally said after calming down, "I...I just wasn't ready for this. I don't want to say goodbye. I don't know how to."

With little else to articulate, we all took turns hugging each other with heavy and reluctant arms. We then separated, with Plato and me on one side and Squatty and JuJu on the other like someone drew a line in the dirt between us.

"You guys have no idea what you've done for me," admitted Squatty, "You couldn't imagine what you two mean to me. I hope we can meet again, but I fear we won't. Let us at least try to stay in touch."

JuJu pulled his stare from the ground and looked me in the eyes, slowly nodding his head with Squatty's words.

"Plato," said Squatty, "I wrote something for you last night."

He pulled out a folded piece of paper from his back pocket and handed it to him.

"Please, read it later, perhaps when you get back to New York."

"Of course," replied Plato thoughtfully.

With disbelief and quiet protest, I crawled onto my motorcycle with a sadness that was just barely starting to break through the transparent borders of my reality. Plato, after hopping on his, looked at Squatty's mother and smiled.

"Say a prayer for us at church this morning, will ya, Suzi?"

"Consider it already done, Plato," said she, smiling in return.

As we reached the end of the driveway, I turned back to wave goodbye one more time. I expected to see Squatty crying, but he wasn't. His expression was sad and solemn, just like his mother's and just like mine. I then looked to JuJu and discovered his face was covered in tears. He was sobbing incessantly. As Plato and I pulled out onto the highway, JuJu clutched Squatty's leg for support and fell to one knee as his walking staff fell to the ground in front of him. He then buried his tear soaked face into Squatty's pants.

As we got up to speed and Squatty's home was no longer in sight, I began to sob as well. The loud engines of the motorcycles just managed to drown out the cries that I produced and the hurt that I screamed. My tears were perhaps exacerbated by so many things occurring in my little life, including Mary, but right at that moment, they exceeded all else from saying goodbye to very rare, very wonderful, and infinitely precious friends.

11

Plato and I decided that our next destination would be Chicago, for it was there the smooth back of the black snake called Route 66 ended, and as good roads were so rare in 1930, time and the beating of our bikes and bodies would be much conserved. There would also be waiting for us in Chicago a direct and daily train into New York City. Plato mentioned he knew the Windy City quite well, and had friends there who would be more than eager to return the motorcycles to Los Angeles on a moment's whim. So our premeditated goal proved to be the first and only one on this trip to have a satisfactory and sound terminus.

With the sting still very fresh from the detachment of Squatty and JuJu, we kept our heads down and our speed up, perhaps hoping the further we distanced ourselves, the less we would miss them. The theory proved a terrible failure, but at the very least we made excellent time. We hardly took a moment to eat during our journey between Oklahoma and Illinois, supplying all the necessary nourishment to our bodies, I suppose, by feeding mostly on our thoughts.

On one particular stop to refuel, and as Plato was inside paying the bill, I happened to catch a crow out of the corner of my eye, flying by close to the other side of the fuel pump from where I leaned against my motorcycle. He was carrying a rather large piece of bread in his beak, soaring low and clean, scanning his mercurial environment for a place to nourish his meal.

Not moments behind, a half dozen other crows were hot on his tail with clear thoughts of the same meal as their own, and before long, the distance between the have and have-nots shortened, if only from the sheer weight and wind drag of the oversized staff of life. After a few taunts and caws and tightly and magnificently executed maneuvers, a vicious battle ensued in mid-air and plain sight, with aerial acrobatics in blitz-krieg and dog-fight fashion. The cherished prize fell from beak to beak, dropping lower and lower out of the sky until the entire production was lost behind the tree line of a small hill.

Plato walked out of the gas station just in time to miss it all, and looked at me with curiosity at what could be so interesting at a place in the middle of nowhere. I shrugged my shoulders at him and waived off my expression, keeping the event to myself and suppressing the energy I had towards it. As much of a performance that it was and how very fortunate I felt for being lucky enough to witness it, I couldn't help be reminded of the similar battles and dog-fights that occur on ground level. I do not refer to the crows of course, but by those of us who are among the wingless; and where even fewer have winged thoughts (thus being grounded twice over) and how, just like the crows, there is more than enough to go around. I at once reflected upon my own life and realized that the brilliance of my childhood was that I had almost everything I needed and almost nothing I wanted. I became suspiciously aware that with little effort and forethought, no one in this world would ever need and no one would ever want. Plato of course would counter this by saying,

So difficult to stray man from greed
So close do we align want with need

The moon was not quite full the evening we arrived in Chicago, but it coruscated as if it were. Along with the city lights, I felt as though we were entering a granulated ghost of a haunting day that lived many years ago and somehow was wrongly accused to be cursed for eternity to envelop the city. The clouds were fluttered across the entire sky like hasty off-white and careless paint strokes, as if the artist were more hungry for dinner at the time than he was for a masterpiece. But I noticed these feathered clouds were strangely keeping their distance from the moon's aim at earth. It seemed as though they were almost scared to cross its path, and as so, helped the moon form its own artificial ring, or halo, mystifying its observers by magnifying the conflicting forces of the known and unknown, and reminding those who witnessed it what real beauty was.

Chicago was indeed a wonderful and polluted place, but just like each city that we visited in South America proved to fall short of Rio de Janeiro, so too had each city we visited in the United States turned out to be a subpar New York.

Being so filthy and sleep starved that evening, I hardly took time to look around. Plato found us a room for the night and after washing up and taking inventory of the dwindling clean clothes in my suitcase, I crawled immediately into bed. As tired as my body was, it was only appropriate to think of thoughtless thoughts, and as a question for Plato formed, I was too exhausted to censor myself to ask it.

"Plato?"

"Yes, Paul."

"Do you think you should be famous?" I questioned, like I was in grade school. "I feel like you should be. I feel like everyone should know you."

Plato laughed.

"No, Paul, I don't," he responded, still laughing through his words.

"Why?"

"Well..." Plato paused, perhaps trying to find words at my level of intelligence to help me better understand. "Through thought and circumstance, I was exceedingly fortunate to discover my own insignificance at a very young age, and therefore have peculiar expectations of myself and the world I live in. Obtaining this wisdom has proven useful, for hardly ever am I disappointed. Others, I am certain, have not discovered their own yet, and are often ruined by their acquisitive perspectives. Subsequently, when it comes to life, I'm afraid if I'm found to be infinitely successful, it is only because I don't care to be."

Once again I had nothing to say but much to think. My thoughts were briefly interrupted by another happy laugh from Plato.

"Nothing is perfect though," he said, "except perhaps a child's laugh. For my view of the universe is not so narrow as others, and what could be triumphant to me may indeed be a considerable failure to most."

I tried to give out a laugh but for reasons of thought, I couldn't make a sound.

"And," said Plato, like he conducted and was now concluding the one-sided conversation for the night, "I suppose that is why I don't think anyone should be famous, ever, or not until long after death, and perhaps not even then. Evolution takes three steps backwards when one has fame, both of himself and his audience. It all promotes the unlisted sin of importance."

Upon first entering that hotel room, I was ready to easily sleep three days of my life away; but after washing clean and settling as snug as a bug in a comfortable bed, Plato's words made me feel like I had slept for weeks and at the same time hadn't slept in months. Neither my mind nor body could lie still. I waited impatiently to assure Plato was sleeping, then quietly got dressed, slipped out the door and went for a walk.

My sojourn was short-lived but instructive, and as I returned to the room, I paused at the door before entering to gather the thoughts I had carefully strewn over the streets of Chicago. I deduced from them that there was no greater sadness than the day a man discovers his own insignificance. What a lonely moment it proves to be. What an infinite moment! This evening, I *uncovered mine*. I always had a haunting suspicion that I was inferior to myself; that is, my perceived self; as most undoubtedly are, and was indirectly and almost innocently knocked unconscious from Plato's brief yet mind-searing words. As somewhat jealous now as I was of those who have not yet discovered their own; or, better still, simply believe it to be untrue, I also realized that my newly found insignificance was an invaluable and irreconcilable necessity of a contented existence. Almost as quickly and soundly as the lock of the hotel room door was released, so was I.

~

"By the way," smiled Plato after kicking my bed a few times the following morning to wake me up, "Welcome to Chicago. This, so I'm told, is where I was born. This, so I remember, is where I grew up."

I rubbed my eyes toward the sliver of sharp light that entered through the window curtains.

"You mean, Chicago? This city is your home?" I responded, like we had just found the ruins of Atlantis.

"It used to be, anyway," he said, laughing again at me and my expressions. "Depending on when the train for New York leaves, if we have time, I'll show you around a bit."

My surroundings transformed instantly. I turned wide awake like someone had dumped a bucket of ice cubes under my sheets. The feeling I had of being in just another wonderful but busy city changed with them as well. It was as if Plato had flipped a switch on the lenses of my eyes, and I had transcended into some sort of holy land. The feeling was lurid yet even, and I sensed that I was now standing on sacred ground.

We first met up with two of Plato's friends on a side street near the northern part of the city. They appeared more excited to see Plato than I was last fall after going a summer without him.

"It's so great to see you, Jon!" said one of them, as they both took turns enthusiastically shaking his hand.

"Same here, boys," replied Plato, "Thanks so much for returning these things."

"No worries," said the other with a wink, "It's always good to get away now and then."

After we unloaded our luggage and Plato gave directions and the name of the bar in Los Angeles, and warnings of the motorcycles' undeserving owners, the two said their farewells in perfect etiquette, hopped on the bikes and disappeared around the corner.

"Well," said I with only a slight sigh of relief, "One more check off the list. Now what?"

Plato smiled at me and then turned his attention across the street. I followed his eyes to find a somewhat small, but well-stocked bookstore that took up the first two floors of a six or so story brick building. The large windows on each floor of the bookstore were framed and covered in heavy crown moldings of a darkly stained hardwood; and every trim, nook, corner and crevice of the bookstore, outside and in, was also outlined with this same and excellent craftsmanship. To me, it looked like a medieval library one would find in a well-preserved castle of Europe.

Plato walked by me without saying a word, crossed the street and entered the bookstore. Like the loyal JuJu with his Squatty, I followed obsequiously, and as the huge doors shut behind me, the first thing I noticed was the wonderful and blended smell of old and new books. One could almost taste the aged leather and inked paper. The acoustics were amazing as well, for anything audible was absorbed so thoroughly by all the books and rich woodwork, that even the sound of my steps became silent by the time they reached my ears. It was almost by instinct to whisper there, for it seemed that the more volume one added to one's voice, the more understanding was lost in articulation and form.

"Hey," said Plato in a well-trained librarian tone, "Follow me. I want to show you something."

He led me toward the back of the store to one of the four large and free standing support pillars of the first floor. Each of the square support pillars of the room was wrapped in book shelves from floor to ceiling and were identically sized and spaced from each other. This particular pillar was identified with a small wooden sign that read, '*Classics*.' I watched as Plato slowly nosed over the books as if he were smelling the knowledge they contained.

"This section is my favorite," he said, "It holds some of the oldest and most cherished books in the store."

I looked at each book with careful awe and respect, walking slowly around the pillar until I met up with Plato on the opposite side of him from where I started.

"I've never seen books like this," I said to him, gently and thoughtfully stroking the leather bindings on the shelf in front of us, "Their contents,

I'm sure, are amazing, but the books themselves are breathtaking."

"True on both accounts," said Plato with a soft smile.

He then stretched his neck a little to see if anyone else was in the bookstore, and after seeing no one, he quietly turned his attention to the shelf at the level of our knees.

"Let's see if the current owners have found this place yet."

Plato turned his palm up toward the ceiling and reached under the shelf like he had performed the maneuver a thousand times. A soft 'click' was almost inaudibly heard.

"You might want to take a half step back, Paul," he whispered.

For a split second, my eyes were playing tricks on me, for I thought the building was collapsing upon us. The entire bookcase that we were facing began to slowly and soundlessly pivot towards us, hinging on one side, and instead of a half step back, I pivoted myself as if to make a run for the door. Plato gently grabbed my elbow before I could launch.

"Look," he said.

His hand disappeared into the darkness that laid behind the now open bookcase and flipped a switch. The secret room of marvelous and highly detailed woodwork was illuminated, and the intricate crown molding and corbels from the ceiling led the eye down to a desk that was loaded with ornately carved leaves and birds and fruit. Nothing was spared in the detail of this small study that was less than the width and length of my own wingspan; from the articulated acorn drawer pulls, to the rose pedal lined book shelves that fortified each wall. If Plato had told me it took three master carpenters over ten years to complete, I would have declared it a miracle that it was finished so quickly, for there was more than a lifetime involved in what I saw. The extremely old books that existed within this closet were so comfortably placed and planned, I wondered if the makers measured them first and built the room around them accordingly.

Thus, as it were, the secret vault was a library within a library.

"This is where my thoughts formed," whispered Plato, "Where ideas were molded and ignited; where my insignificance was established, and where my *self* was disowned. This is where I called home, and where I spent almost all of my days and nights for nearly ten years."

As usual I said nothing and only let my ears and eyes take in what they almost didn't believe.

"Little is it known and much is it denied," continued he, "But wisdom is often stunted by education. It sometimes suffocates the intellect, and even though I was surrounded by endless amounts of knowledge and thought, in time I resisted the words of these books and yielded to the temptation of my own. I spent most days within these walls staring into the silence of darkness to allow my own *nous* to breathe."

When I finally thought I was able to speak, or more like produce sounds, I was only able to say, "How....magnificent."

"The only thing magnificent was how lucky I was when he discovered us," responded Plato.

I questioned him with a wordless glance.

"The owner of this bookstore. Come, let me show you one last thing, and then we have a train to catch."

Plato led me back out onto the street and we turned immediately down an alley that paralleled the bookstore. At the end of it rested a heaping mound of trash that exponentially smelled worse and worse the closer we got to it, and by the time Plato finally stopped, his toes were at its edge, and the fumes from this manmade hill were unbearable. He then began to look it over with a resourceful and almost nostalgic expression.

"After my mother left us, my father rented a room above this bookstore. He was not a good man at any time in my life, but when my mother wasn't there to stand between us, things only got worse. Anyway, this was our hiding spot. He couldn't stomach to come looking for us in here, no matter how much he had to drink."

By now I had the front of my shirt covering most of my face, with my nose buried as deep as I could get it into the crook of my elbow. But my shirt and my shirtsleeve did little to filtrate the exhaust from this hummock of trash.

"Thou shallow Time," said Plato, in a different tone, "Thou shallow and swift turn Thy take."

The smell had now penetrated my being, and my eyes began to sting as my sinuses became full, and even though my senses of smell and taste were preoccupied with the pungent pile, my *mind sense* wasn't. It remained clear and fresh, and I perceived that this place may have been where Plato had hidden, and where he had fallen to perhaps the lowest point in his life; but I could tell it was also, and much more importantly, the place where he had risen from.

"We didn't always make it to this cover, though," he continued, "Sometimes he caught us at the door here, and beat us thoroughly for our attempt at escape. It was one of these times when Harold, the owner of the bookstore, discovered us, and let that little hidden room of his become our new hiding spot. He often had food waiting for us there as well as books upon piles of books to read."

Plato, again, showed no signs of crying or being upset in any way, similar to the moment in Squatty's barn just a couple of days before. However, his words were full of cold emotion.

"*Us*?" I said, questioning his continued use of plurality.

"Oh," admitted Plato, realizing his memory, "I guess I never told you about my sister."

"You... have a sister?" I responded, still not yet fully recovered from Plato sharing the fact that we were in his hometown.

"Yes. A twin sister, to be more precise."

Plato then turned and looked out to the end of the alley. The traffic had picked up on the street since we first arrived and I watched with Plato the cars that pestered by like black flies in New Hampshire during the month of May. As I was trying to imagine this twin sibling of Plato's and how amazing she must be, and how, perhaps beautiful she was, on all fronts, if only half the caliber person her brother was, Plato severed my thoughts directly.

"I should say I *had* a sister," he whispered.

He raised a clenched fist up to his mouth and pressed it firmly against his lips.

"She took her own life, out there, on the street."

The city noise was muted in an instant. I felt tears form on my bottom eyelids before I could understand what was being said. Plato's eyes, and tone for that matter, remained dry, but his armor cracked a great deal more in his stature and looked almost ready to fall off him.

"Our neighborhood took part in a city-wide parade that honored the veterans of the war in Europe," he slowly continued, "My father fought over there as well, and was asked to don his uniform and march with the others that morning. When the small parade passed this bookstore, the streets were lined with spectators clapping and cheering with gratitude, that is, until the moment my sister landed on the street."

Plato paused and subtlety steadied himself. He then lifted his eyes and pointed to the top of the bookstore building.

"She jumped from that corner there and landed only inches from my father as he was marching by."

My entire being was straining. As much as I resisted my imagination, the event Plato described was playing out before me, and I felt as though I was there that same morning with him.

"Where were you?" I whispered, wanting to know more, but not wanting to hear it.

"I was up there too, standing right beside her. We climbed to the roof to get a better view of the parade, and as soon as we identified our father in the sea of uniforms passing by, she turned to me and said, 'I love you, brother,' and stepped off the cornice. There was no warning, no sign. Not even the smallest hint had I ever detected of her intentions. My only reaction was to reach for her, and the very tips of my fingers grazed a few strands of her beautiful reddish-brown hair, but nothing else."

I pressed the palm of my hand to my forehead, trying to contain and decipher the information that was being put into it.

"And as a final blow to my father," Plato said evenly, "It also just happened to be his birthday. My sister wanted to make sure he would never forget that day."

The air had long turned heavy and thick since we had stepped outside of the bookstore, but now I found myself unable to move in it. My breath was labored and my eyelids were consciously forced to blink.

"Even so," concluded he, "To this day she is still my confidant, my consultant. She is my best friend. She is the only one I know that understood the concept of time."

The quiet cab ride to the train station was as silent and bated as much as it was ruminative. Plato's childhood stories were so horrific to me that they entered my mind as some sort of foreign entity. It was almost as if they weren't real. Certainly for Plato, it was a large drop of poison in the aqueduct of his being; and although it was not enough to decimate, it sickened and saddened those organs that were never designed or meant to be hurt. The recovery of his childhood, although never to be fully cured, had simmered slowly. His intricate world that continued to be exposed, infected me collaterally with hurt in turn, from which, like a sibling of both his sister and him, I have still yet to recover. Compared to my nearly fairytale upbringing, I couldn't understand the idea of them, and as a safeguard, applied and stored their thoughts as if they happened to some distant stranger on the other side of the world. It seemed as though Plato had similar views on where he placed these memories as well, for besides the fact that the old bookstore owner left him everything after he died, we hardly mentioned the city of Chicago again.

As Plato and I were sitting there in the busy station waiting for the train to New York City, a wonderfully cute and dark mouse appeared out from beneath the bench we sat on, scurrying right by my shoe, and, after the slightest hesitation, as though looking both ways before he leaped, proceeded to zigzag in and out and around the heavy foot traffic that trampled the platform. Defying all odds, and with more luck and fear on his side than skill and talent, it took him nearly a full minute to make the twelve or so foot journey, darting forward, then backward, then sideways, then running with traffic, then against it, and back around again with the utmost unchecked and nervous energy. He disappeared over the side and onto the tracks just as our train was pulling in, and I feared after all that effort he was finally squished by the train like the copper pennies my childhood friends and I would lay on the tracks for the oncoming trains that charged through our hometown. But Lady Luck was still clinging to his back, for I saw a glimpse of him on the other side as he paused to catch his breath and nibble the scrap of food he had in his mouth, and, after looking back at me and his triumphant journey with a humble yet glorified glance of victory, he went on his merry way to live another day. I nearly wanted to stand up and cheer for the little creature, but instead kept myself still and restrained my enthusiasm. I compromised my reaction with a silent and smiling sigh of relief toward his dramatic escape, and wondered what on earth he was thinking to attempt such a life threatening adventure. The only thing plausible for his actions was the food between his teeth, as if he risked life and limb in order to sustain life and limb. I imagined trying to be in his situation but failed directly, as I realized for the first time that I had never been without food for more than half a day in my life. And then, for contentions I could not translate but knew were tethered, I wondered what the world was for.

In an attempt to conclude our visit to Chicago, I asked Plato if he ever missed his hometown.

"If my math is correct," I said, "You haven't been back here in almost three years. I have trouble being outside of New Hampshire for less than three weeks."

"Nah," shrugged Plato, "The only thing I miss is..."

"Hello Jonathan," came a voice from behind us, "I heard you were in town but didn't believe it. But, alas, here you are."

She smiled like a child and then tilted her head at Plato as if she was a puppy trying to understand a command. I knew instantly that this girl and Plato had a past.

"Good morning, Victoria," replied Plato with sprinkled hesitation, "News travels fast around here."

Initially, Victoria's appearance was quietly astonishing to me. She was not something one would find living under a bridge, by any means, but I dare say she had little to offer in what one would perhaps generally consider the qualities of attraction. One could describe her, from appearance alone, as a uniquely beautiful creature in a very peculiar way, but in the purest form of honesty, this description may easily be accused of being a bit of an exaggeration. Although it would not be anywhere near a flat-out lie, perhaps just a tiny hint of a stretch; and more times than not would be questioned by the one observing, as well as the eye of the beholder, in any dim or direct light.

But it was her animation that would sell one's soul for a sixpence, and the more she spoke and the more her voice was heard, the more I forgot her physicality. The mole on her upper lip, her bent, bumpy and slightly offset nose, her rather oversized and lobe-less ears, her hair that matted flat and lifeless to her head on almost every side, as well as her stocky build and heavy set legs, disappeared almost instantly from my eyes. When I first heard her, it almost felt like I was coming from a very cold outside to a very warm within. I felt safe and sound, as if submersing in a hot drawn bath as her vocal cords encompassed and heated my bones and blood. Only one word came to mind after watching her mouth form sounds and sentences: *seduction*.

The street maintenance or building construction crews of New York City that I overheard catcalling endlessly to the pretty women that walked by them as they worked, would not perhaps call on Victoria, but to be sure, if she were to call on them, -as she easily would on a bet, for she seemed fearless in all considerations of life-they would be struck dumb at her suggestiveness, and perhaps become anxious or nervous at the very sound of her. The crews, as outspoken as when they were born, would then go mute, and quietly think of her for the rest of their workday, go home and kiss their wives goodnight, and lay awake in bed with thoughts of her still stuck stubbornly in their heads, with high hopes of them seeing her somehow again.

The sparks that flashed across her eyes with each word she dropped from her mouth reminded me of a violent beauty, like summer lightning storms that lit up the sky, and being in her presence I could think of not one living creature that was more attractive in the world. Seeing her from across a crowded room, or at that very train station, I would not have given her a look, let alone a second one. But now, in close proximity, and while eavesdropping on her conversation with Plato, I found that I couldn't pull my eyes away from her. It wasn't that silly and mundane physical attraction that the world over falls for, but it was something else. Perhaps the French would describe it as *je nais se quoi*, but I think for me she was bursting at the seems with plain ol' fashioned feminine fervor.

And finally after all this, my eyes led me back to her form, and it revealed such confidence and womanly allure at the deepest of levels, and became so attractive compared to just a few moments before, that I felt myself turning to putty without even earning a glance from her.

"Well, I'm afraid I just wanted to see you in the flesh," she said with a giggle, as I realized I missed their entire conversation due to my selfish and offset thoughts of her, "And so I have, and you look better than ever."

"You too, Vick," Plato responded with a much more conservative laugh of his own.

They embraced warmly and as the train whistle blew, their lips met in restrained emotion.

"Goodbye, Jonathan," she said.

"Goodbye, Amore."

"What a mind she has," whispered Plato to himself as Victoria twisted on her heels and walked away from us. He readily noticed that I was inflicted and stupefied by her presence too.

"Sorry, Paul," he said solemnly, "I didn't even think to introduce you two. If it's any consolation, you may rest assured that you are not the only one in this world who has sustained a broken heart."

She was nearly lost in the crowd of people as Plato and I watched her slowly disappear in them. He placed his open hand firmly over his chest and yelled to her.

"Vide cor meum! Vide cor tuum!" *

**Translation: Here is my heart! Here is your heart*

Before boarding the train, I noticed a mail post in the station and sent one last letter to Mary concluding the summer of 1930:

My Immortal Beloved,

The moment is always young
Regardless of years
The song is always sung
In spite of all fears.
But a moment remembering moments
Can prove the fondest of all
As immortal as the heavens
Though the heavens may fall.

Paul

12

Upon returning to NYU, I was greeted by four of five letters that Mary mailed to me over the course of the summer. A couple of them are included below:

Dearest Sweetheart,

Currently in Nassau. Boys chase girls more here than back home, if you can believe that, but it's still all the same. Without knowing you exist, the silly boys try to be you but none of them are. All of them together in the world could not equal one half of you. No one comes close. No one ever could.

I look for you when we are out at sea, for I heard before I left that we were headed in the same direction. I find myself hoping each ship I see is carrying you.

I would teach you how to forget me if I knew how to do the same with you. I would teach you forgiveness too, if only I knew how to forgive myself.

Mary

Dearest Sweetheart,

Perhaps you are currently finding the same, but time aboard a ship allows for extended thinking. Real and honest thinking. I have discovered that with your absence came a slow and subtle restriction. I was physically tied to you; bound up by all the ropes and fasteners of you. There was no doubt I was in a position I never wanted to get out of, but you had tied a knot I couldn't loosen. I didn't want to escape, but felt like I couldn't even if given the choice. There, I found, was the rub. Like a restrained appendage, it reached a point where I could hardly move, or at times, could hardly feel. The worst of it all was that you were far and away.

It wasn't until this lonely summer of sea air that I realized it was the other way around. It was I who tied myself to you, tied the impossible knot I couldn't untie, and continued to squeeze tighter and tighter, never wanting to let go; all the while thinking it was you who was suffocating me, when I was the one choking myself.

Mary

The most recent one was dated just a few days before I got back, and lasted only as long as a sentence, being as direct in nature as it was in brevity.

I want nothing more now and for the rest of my life than for us to be together.

I did not allow any inkling of hope or joy to enter my heart, as much as it was begging for it, and even though the rest of me had succumbed at the thought of being back with Mary, when I sat down to respond, the words I left on the paper disquieted and disheartened me.

Dearest Mary,

I hold your letters in my hands as delicately as I held your gentle and percussioned breaths in my lungs when we used to lie on the riverbank and you fell asleep in my arms. I imagine now that your hands are holding these letters with me and we are reading them together aloud; as we allow it only through brief discipline and only when our urges are restrained from the soft and several, pitter-pattered kisses we exchange.

I don't want to meet another soul for the rest of my life. I regret meeting almost everyone up until now. I only need to know you.

But Mary, please forgive me, for I am still poisoned by our ending to start again, and my tenuous heart is not yet finished being torn and therefore cannot yet mend.

Paul

For the next several months, Mary and I once again went dark and silent, and no letters or contact of any kind was correlated. Emily was once again there to help fill the void in her quirky and provocative way, for she was waiting for me at my dormitory the day after my return, and the day of my first football practice.

"It's about time!" she said, in the cutest smile and in an almost cuter summer dress. She then darted across the room and climbed on me like a squirrel in a tree, "I've been worried sick!"

I hated admitting it to myself, but there was a wonderful comfort seeing her again. It was a very selfish emotion that I was well aware of and enjoyed too much, but as our relationship existed, for the most part innocent, it left little guilt in my conscious.

"Oh, nothing much," said Emily, after I asked her what she did over the summer. "A boy followed me home one afternoon and then proceeded to bring me flowers every day thereafter, and by the end of the first week I was bored to tears with them. Now, after an entire summer's worth of being inundated with flowers, I completely despise them and never want to see another rose petal again!"

"You poor, poor thing," I teased in reply.

Emily gave me a pouty expression and stuck her tongue out at me. I think she despised the fact that I was never once jealous of all her suitors.

"You know," she said, after looking me over with an enticing smirk, "All summer, whenever I imagined doing something or going somewhere, I was not alone. You were always there with me, Paul. Do you have any idea how much torture that was? Do you have even the slightest notion how much that destroyed my freedom? Oh, I just hate you!"

She playfully spun herself away from me with arms crossed and nose in the air.

"Well then," I countered with a matching smirk of my own, "I'm here now. Make the most of me."

~

By the time classes had begun my junior year at NYU, football had long been an afterthought. It innocently got in the way of more and more interesting engagements, and I found myself fully ashamed in the way I felt toward it, for it was so very important to me for so long. Up until the not-so-distant past, nothing was more vital to my existence. There was little else that mattered. Not for a second did I think that I had wasted my youth on the trivial sport, but I did acknowledge to myself how things would be slightly different and how my time would be employed otherwise if I had the chance to do it all over again.

Those very particular engagements that so interested me, of course, most always involved Plato, or sometimes Emily, and sometimes but rarely all three of us; yet I also found that I was venturing off alone much more often. It was very much a new and exhilarating experience for me. Realizing the unaccustomed and tantalizing art of being by myself, I also began to discover and think of things on my very own. It was an almost awkward feeling to allow myself to look at the world from different angles. In a way, I was relearning things I already thought I knew. I dare say I established and honed these perspective skills during this time, which I applied to and for the rest of my life.

Plato encouraged this behavior in his own way without directly mentioning a word of it. One day at Washington Square, I teased him about how he should be the ruler of this planet, primarily because he would be the best and perhaps only real candidate, and at the very least, he would be in a position to meet all the great and famous people of the world.

"I think the world runs on opinion and nothing else, as it is so easily influenced," he laughed in response, "Facts are like unanswered prayers; only with less conviction. Very few people, if any, who are considered great and famous should be great and famous. For the most part, we lionize the wrong lions and lambast the wrong lambs."

"But surely one or two of them have earned the title," I replied without any facts or names that came to mind.

"Perhaps," he shrugged, "But similar to every great story one hears, ten go untold. So, too, is it with those that are considered great."

"You mean I could be sitting next to someone great right now on this park bench and not even know it?" I joked.

"I wouldn't go that far," Plato said, ignoring my humor and rolling his eyes, "But I think I've met a few who would qualify."

"Tell me of one," I pleaded, like a child who just crawled in bed for the night not anywhere near ready for sleep or their parent to leave them.

Plato thought a bit, with his eyes darting back and forth, as if scanning the depths of his mind, mentally thumbing through the files of his memory.

"Well, I know of this man who decided to be less of a burden to his family and himself by finding a tree and living in it," he began, "After fashioning this make-shift fort in the backwoods of his neighbor's property, which sat high above the ground and upwards at the very near top of the tree, his existence became almost instantly free and clear. His one and only companion was a small potbelly stove that barely fit both him and it in the floor plan, his mansion being so large. It would eventually prove to come in handy on those cold and bitter northern midwest winter nights, or so he assumed. There he lived, growing fast accustomed to his independence; and so happy with his burden-less way of life that when the leaves did fall and the cold air slowly crept in, he found it unnecessary to bother his stove or the firewood at the base of the tree to keep him warm. Because he did not waste energy of himself, he did not wish to waste energy of anything else, it being only fair, so, for five months kept the little potbellied stove warmer than it kept him. To this day I understand he is still there, maintaining little or no impact on anything or anyone including himself. To hear that he moved back to his family's dwelling would make no difference to me and my view of him; for even to attempt this type of elevated existence requires greatness. And of all the so-called great people living in this world; of all their great successes and fame and monies and accomplishments; of all the leaders or scientists or intellects who have supposedly advanced mankind and who most would like to meet, this man who lives in a tree, unknown to almost everyone, is at the very top of my list. For he, among all others, is the most advanced and the one who could elevate mankind to where it needs to be: self-reliant, self-content, and munificently free."

~

As for Emily, we did not spend all of our time together laughing and giggling. Our moments did not always consist of her throwing kisses and me dodging them, or me trying not to get caught eyeing her flawless little figure. We exchanged serious and thoughtful moments too. I once asked about her family, which only included her mother, to which gravity immediately took hold of her face and body in multiples.

"My mother died when I was thirteen," she said, trying to balance her emotions, "From a silly cut on her ankle from a rusty nail. It was too late when she finally agreed to receive treatment for it. I loved her so, and, if possible, I think she loved me more."

"I…" was all I was allowed before she interrupted me.

"Say, do you believe in ghosts?" she asked, delaying her emotions with anticipation for an answer.

"I've always wanted to," I said as I set my head back just as she set hers forward in synchronized movements, "But, I've yet to meet one. It is unlike religion for me. I seem to always want a bit of sound evidence or proof."

She appeared somewhat satisfied with my answer and shrugged her eyebrows with half apathy and half sadness as she kept her eyes steady on mine.

"I feel like my mother is always here," Emily said evenly, "I have no proof of it, but I also don't require any either."

"Well," I replied trying to lighten the air, "It seems as though my mother is always haunting me wherever I go, and she's still living."

Emily gave out a loud but short laugh to my response, but also as if she just remembered an experience that matched my statement.

"Gosh I love cemeteries," she said, shifting around subjects, "Is that weird?"

"No, I like them too. But make no mistake, you are still very weird in general."

"What is *your* mother like, Paul?"

"I guess she's wonderful, in so many ways," I said, being vaguely honest.

"My mother used to say to me all the time that nothing was fair in this world, like she was giving an excuse for herself and all of human behavior," said Emily with a nostalgic expression, "And though I never did, whenever she said that, I always wanted to respond to her, 'But mother, it doesn't mean we should stop trying to be fair.'"

I was so impressed by her words that for a moment I thought I was talking to Plato. We kept quiet for some moments longer until I figured I had one more thing to add about my mother.

"Perhaps the biggest difference between my mother and me," I said with a truthful innocence, "Is that she thinks everything is so important when it doesn't have to be."

Emily then laughed harder than I have ever heard her laugh before.

"My dearest Paul!" she sang, "You may have identified and solved the problem with the human race!"

~

Before leaving New York City for Christmas break that winter, I visited a few stores to get some last minute holiday shopping in for my family. As I was walking by one of their window displays, I noticed a beautiful harmonica. Instantly I thought of Squatty, and although I barely had enough money to afford it, or rather, not enough, I bought it anyway with a small loan from Plato. I sent it directly to Oklahoma with appropriate postage and instruction to further it to Rio if he and JuJu had headed to South America already. With any luck he would hopefully receive it in time for the holiday.

And yet Squatty must have been on the same wavelength of thought, for upon arriving home, my mother told me a package had been delivered for me earlier that day. I opened the perfectly wrapped box to find a beautiful new football. A small note was taped to one end written in flawless penmanship:

Paul,

Thanks for putting up with me and my dreams of being a football star.

Merry Christmas and a Happy 1931!
Squatty

13

It wasn't until the end of winter break did Mary and I finally run into each other. This was purely by chance and circumstance, but the scales were tipped in our favor due almost entirely to our small town restrictions and the handful of traditions our youth allowed.

Thus the outdoors was our only venue and although it was still a bit early in the winter season, a couple of buddies and I grabbed our ice skates and headed down to the Connecticut River. We had already experienced a few bone chilling spells that year. In the past our seasonal river skating had usually waited well into the first freezer days of February, depending on how low the mercury dropped. But this time around, for whatever reason, (perhaps because cabin fever had set in early), our skate laces were being tied up the second week of January. It was also just two days shy of when I was to return to New York City.

My friends and I were not the only ones having similar thoughts, for it was here that Mary and I made eye contact for the first time in nearly a year, as she was already at the river that afternoon with mutual friends when I arrived. Someone must have scouted the river and let the secret out, for all of us had the same goal of scratching up the perfectly smooth and virgin ice that completely covered our annual playing field; stretching from shore to shore, smartly trimming the cutaneous skinned coastlines as if by design, like a freshly and over-tightened drum. For two or three months out of the year, we had land where there was none before, and we made the most of a rare property that was forever unoccupied and unowned.

Mary's hair had grown tremendously quick from when I last saw her. It was sticking out almost bashfully from the bottom of her hat and I briefly smiled at how wonderful it was to see it again. She was sitting on the river's bank in a cradled couch of snow, unaware yet of my presence, trying to tighten her laces in considerable frustration. I gave out a short but audible laugh remembering how she hated to tie her own skates, for she could never quite get them tight enough, and as a result, always had me do it for her. For some reason I loved to tie her skates, like a father dressing his child for the first day of school, and it reminded me of what Plato once told me: 'An old and excellent forgotten feeling that has been suddenly *re-felt*, can often surpass any other new and wonderful experience the mind has to offer. It makes human life worth living with the chance to alter reality and replicate the experience as if novel, even if it is already registered in the memory.'

This briefly forgotten memory of Mary certainly qualified as one, and although this difficulty was not funny to her, she made up for it once these skates became secure and vertical and placed upon frozen water. She moved like a serpent with blades on its belly, like she had been born feet first with skates on. She out-skated most of the boys and certainly all of the girls we knew of and grew up with.

"Here," I said walking up to her as she was kicking one of her heels into the snow from losing patience, "Allow me the honor of doing that for you."

We both smiled warmly at each other, almost shyly without saying a word; as if we were both stunned at our joy of seeing each other and relieved at each other's joy for the same reason.

"Thank you, kind stranger," Mary said, in her coquettishly silly and serious way.

In the blink of an eye, Mary was out on the ice like a bird set free from a cage. Our group of about seven or eight had halfway acquired our ice legs in the general area until someone suggested we all skate up river. Three of the girls that came with Mary turned down the offer with complaints of being too cold, as it was indeed *very* cold, but the rest of us shouldered into the headwind, not willing to admit to each other and our New England stubbornness that we wanted to do the same as those girls and head home as well.

But before long the entire group had soon turned back. Mary and I were the only ones left as if secretly planned by her friends, or mine, or the Gods. I turned to her with a nonchalant look as if to continue further up the river, for if we stood there looking at each other much longer we would be forced to talk and being odd strangers to each other, we were both uncomfortable and equally not ready for conversation.

"It's not that cold out," she snickered, and pushed gracefully off her skates and headed North once again into the headwind.

Mary could literally skate circles around me. She possessed the legs of a ballerina and the balance of a tightrope walker without any dedicated practice that was required of each. She effortlessly polished out the jagged lines that whisked by her on the winter shorelines and the barren trees that shot up on the mountainsides and beyond; for all things seem to smoothen as she passed and those of us that witnessed her move on the ice were calmed and courted and cooed as well.

My legs were too far primed and pruned for football, and although I had decent balance and coordination, I was at most an effective yet highly inefficient skater. To watch me skate would be similar to watching me fall out of an airplane with no parachute, in hopes to defy gravity and the pending ground. In spite of all this and thanks for the most part to my unyielding determination as well as Mary's patience with a slower pace, I was able to keep up with her.

We continued for some time and when the sun was near ready to set, as we were well into the short days of winter, we came upon a straightened stretch of the river. The long and wooden covered bridge that connected Vermont with New Hampshire could barely be seen off in the distance. I had closed the gap between the two of use to a point where I could reach out and almost hold Mary's hand. Holding hands was my only goal from the start of our journey, for I loved to hold her hand doing anything, and sadly could not remember when the last time I did so. But before I was about to do just that, I heard myself instinctively yell to her, "*Open water*!"

I don't know if Mary had let her mind wander far off from where she was, or that she was distracted by watching the steel blue sky slowly darken, but she hardly slowed down as she headed straight for the opening in the ice, and like Plato reaching for his sister atop the bookstore building, I reached for Mary in a similar way with similar results, and she fell through the thinned ice like a stone.

Veering off from the opening, I spun in a tight circle to return to it. I impulsively dove head first on the ice and slid on my belly as far as it would take me. Mary's little red mitten was all I could see above the water level, holding on to a part of the ice that thankfully had yet to break. We were upon a section of the river that had a steeper grade which made for a stronger current, and Mary barely held on from being swept away downstream and under the ice. I reached her little mitten and plunged into the water with both arms far and deep. Gripping her almost by the shoulder, my first instinct from the shock of the freezing water and the unrelenting current was to let go of her. It was so stingingly cold. In an odd and terrifying way, it felt like I was being burned by an open flame.

I have no staying memory of the following few moments, but when I finally came to my senses and my memory began recording again, Mary and I were off the ice and onto the bank. I opened the front of my coat after taking off hers and nestled Mary close to my body with her limbs tightly wrapped around me and her face pressed firmly into my chest. It was getting darker and colder, and I knew I couldn't stay there long. Mary was unresponsive. Her temperature was dropping in direct proportion to the air that surrounded us. She was shivering so violently that I couldn't make her stop, no matter how tight I held her. I was her only source of heat, as her body felt like it gave up producing any of its own. With her wrapped around me like a scarf, I stood to climb up the embankment and into the woods. I briefly looked back to the river opening to see her abandoned red mitten frozen to where she was holding onto the ice.

We kept falling and stumbling due to the steep terrain. My ice skates were still on and although the deep snow aided my balance, I continued to get caught up on roots and branches of the heavy underbrush we hiked through. I remember repeating aloud, over and over the phrase: "*Keep moving.*"

We finally stumbled out onto the railroad tracks, the very same tracks that took me to New York City. My ankles rolled on their sides with each step and were so badly twisted that they eventually went from excruciating pain to almost no pain at all. After a few hundred yards and a few thousand prayers, I saw a light off in the distance, a house light, and upon reaching it the startled man at the door hurried us in without a word and I dropped to my knees in front of his roaring fireplace. Mary's body had literally frozen to mine, or rather melted to it, and with the help of the kind man, it took several minutes to slowly peel her off me.

The man phoned Mary's parents and within an hour they had arrived with clothes and several blankets. After making sure she was throughly layered and insulated with them, we boarded her into the car and headed back to their house. I stayed there at Mary's bedside throughout the night, holding her thawed yet unresponsive hand, and exchanging and heating the warm water bottles that surrounded her. By noon the next day, Mary's mother insisted on me going home for a bath, fresh clothes and much needed rest. Since Mary was sleeping peacefully, I silently slipped away obeying her mother's wishes.

My own parents had gotten wind of the event and when I opened our front door, my mother had a warm bath already drawn and waiting for me. I hobbled into bed thereafter and fell sound asleep. It wasn't until the next morning did I wake and only thanks to my father gently rubbing my back.

"Good morning, Paul," he whispered, "I would have let you sleep longer, but I believe you have a train to catch to New York City."

My ankles were so swollen and sore that when I got up from my bed it felt like I was walking on stilts, but I managed to get packed and ready and with little time to spare, I phoned Mary's house but no one answered. I thought about postponing my return back to NYU to stay longer with her, but remembered that classes started the following day and it was intensely forbidden by my school and my football coach to miss any, especially the first day of them.

My parents dropped me off at the train station with big hugs goodbye. They waved with cold hands but warm smiles as their car drove away, for it was too cold to see me off at the boarding platform. As was my habit, I looked for Mary before stepping onto the train. She wasn't there of course, as I expected, for she was certainly still in bed resting. I absentmindedly reached into my coat pocket only to discover her other red mitten that I placed there after arriving at her parents house. I wondered if the other mitten was still attached to the ice from where Mary held on to it. The little mitten only pacified me for a moment as I looked it slowly over in my hand. I wished I could have at least said goodbye to her, or even received an update from her parents on her recovery. Limping up the first step of the train like an old man that needed a cane, I heard someone call out to me. It was Mary. *My* Mary. The clouded steam from the train cleared out from the platform and she appeared like a Chicago moon.

At once we embraced. Of all the warmth and emotions that flooded my heart, and all the things I had to show her and share with her and all the many things I wanted to tell her, I could only repeat aloud the words, *I love you*. I wanted to miss that train and the rest of my life; to provoke the infinite;

and to be stilled and statued in that moment of us,
that moment of ever.

~

Emily was once again waiting for me at my dormitory room upon my return. As she was very much a part of the unconscious arrogance of youth, she invited herself to my place whenever she felt like it, without once ever asking or even telling me of her plans to do so. Of course her beauty got her away with most things she desired in life, including those that involved me, and I found myself with nothing more to do than to smile at the thought of her forwardness and the almost possessive entitlement she had with anything her eyes cared to fall upon. Thus, as it were, when I opened my door she was safely and soundly asleep in my bed as though she had slumbered there since infancy.

I quietly went over and gently held her hand and whispered her name. She eventually stirred, and from the recognition of my voice a large smile developed on her face. She sighed warmly. I felt a pang in my heart from waking her, as she looked so adorable and content, almost child-like in her expression, and undoubtedly far off in a dream, that when she finally opened her evening eyes and I came into focus, she immediately began to pout, then whimper, then at last turned away from me.

"I'm sorry, Emily," I said, "I didn't want to wake you but I myself need to go to bed."

"It's not that," she replied, muffling her voice under blankets and sheets, "It's the look on your face!"

I sat back a bit from the edge of the bed and wondered what she could possibly be talking about.

"You know what? You boys are all the same! Every one of you pathetic when it comes to us girls. Just look how you are with Mary! Blind devotion! Oh, I *really* hate you, Paul McNamara!"

She bullied her way out of bed with her gorgeous hair all puffed and pressed by my pillow on one half of her head, while the rest of it shot out almost straight on the other half. She looked as if she stood sideways in front of an industrial fan all day. At the doorway and after putting on her winter coat, she burst into tears.

"I won't give up on you, Paul," she said without looking at me, "Something has happened since we last saw each other. I can only assume you are back with Mary. I can tell by the look on your pretty little face. I know I don't have a chance and should abandon all hope, but I refuse to give up! You see, I have a terribly big heart that has unforgivable and irreconcilable timing, and you, in all your hurt-free life have betrayed it! I suppose it is your right as much as it is my fate, but for now, I remain happy, for you are still in my life, and anyone who is truly happy is only then truly beautiful. So there!"

She kicked my door out of frustration and then put her hands on her hips.

"Anyway," she said with reluctance after somewhat regaining her composure, "I left a bunch of kisses on your pillow everyday while you were gone."

She left without saying goodbye, leaving my jaw open, my eyes wide, and my mouth silent without sound. With all the recent events, Emily and her words struck me dumb. For no apparent reason, I sat at the edge of my bed for some time, motionless; with my mind slowly wandering between varying thoughts: some involving beautiful things and beautiful moments, but most were concerned with the fuzzy and distant hum of existence and the mild yet persistent sting of time.

Although I never received a letter from Emily and therefore could not recognize her handwriting, I found an unsigned and undated piece of paper under my pillow the following morning and could only deduce its authorship to her.

Idle days wasted
Tidal waves tasted
Sleepless nights traced with
Petty fears faced with
Final tears pasted
Innocence chasted
Nothing replaced with
Time makes all haste with

~

Plato and I met up a few days later at Washington Square.

"Well, I told you it was going to happen sooner or later," said he, with a hint of indifference after telling him Mary and I were back on again, "Does this mean there will be no more tears and sadness and sullenness on this park bench anymore?"

"Shut up," I said, with a more sarcastic tone than his.

This particular day was rare and mild, especially for where it fell on the calendar, and people were out and about in the city and especially in the park. They all seemed happy and alive, carrying their heads up instead of down, as their usual and hurried pace downshifted to a slackened mosey. Some were feeding the birds of the park that weren't clever enough to fly south for the winter, while others were making snowmen and snowballs, seemingly without a care for time, or dates, or appointments and all that other silly stuff of life the world gets caught up in. Whether the unexpected spike of a few degrees in temperature was to blame, I knew not, but it was wonderful to observe.

"Hey look," interrupted Plato as I was in the middle of bragging about endless love and devotion, "Check out that guy over there having his lunch."

A well-dressed man was sitting alone on a park bench eating. Just as Plato pointed him out to me, a homeless person sat on the same bench as this man. The well-dressed one gave a look of disgust to the not-so-well-dressed other, then quickly gathered his things, got up, and walked away.

"Humph," contemplated Plato, "No offense but I dare say, Paul, you were boring me to tears, and so I was watching that man have his lunch alone, and imagined for him that a beautiful woman would come up beside him, only because he had a look on him that desperately wished it so. And no sooner than I had this thought, I caught this other less fortunate man looking for a seat."

After finally getting over the fact that Plato wasn't incredibly interested in my incredibly interesting tales of romance, I focused my attention on the man on the bench Plato was talking about and how he was sitting there, peaceful as a pear, enjoying the moment and the day like everyone else.

"Now," continued Plato, "As things stand, the well-dressed man who was having his lunch will probably never return to this bench because of what just took place, for as we all know the rich mix with the poor like oil and water. As public as this park is, we are private citizens with our *very* important and imaginary boundaries. But could you imagine if that homeless man had been an attractive woman like I first had hoped for? If she had only sat down for a moment to check her purse or to powder her nose, and only glanced in his direction to acknowledge his existence as she got up and left, the man would return to that very same bench everyday for as long as he could, rain or shine, perhaps eating the same food for good luck, in longing hope to see her again."

With Plato's words, I found myself imagining this poor man sitting on the bench as a beautiful woman.

"Years would go by," he said, "And this man might just revolve his life indirectly around this park for small incidentals, meetings, or lunches, or, depending on where he lived, just for walks after work or dinner, or to read. All in hopes to see the beautiful girl again."

Plato and I both fell silent for only a moment, staring at this poor and innocent man on the bench.

"Say..." I said with an enlightened and suspicious scowl, "Are you making fun of me, Plato? Are you trying to refer to Emily on all this?"

"No, no," laughed Plato from his belly, "I was mostly making fun of myself. Emily is not the only girl in this city, Paul, nor is she the only girl who visits this park. Why else do you suppose I always want to meet up here? Your interest in Emily has only recently and slightly dissipated because you are now back with Mary. But I know that interest in Emily still exists even though you will no doubt deny it. The focus with my girl in this park has only flourished because she interests me terribly, but it may also be from the fact that I have no chance of rekindling the love I had with Victoria."

I had such a hard time agreeing with Plato on this only because he was absolutely and annoyingly correct.

"Call it what you want," he summarized, "but it all depends on time and circumstance."

"And nothing else?" I questioned, not wanting the topic to close.

"Call the world a disappointment," he said thoughtfully, " and so it will become. Call it a tragedy, a lie, or a trick, and so, too, will it be so. But call the world wonderful and fully believe it so, and guess what happens then? At once the evidence is overwhelming, and it, too, becomes as it is demanded, and whatever next you call it or want it to be, no matter where you are or who you're with."

As we are so prone at finding fault, for it is much easier to hate than to love, some may consider Plato as *flaw-ful* instead of flawless. I have no doubt that he would agree with them, but I believe Plato was an ideal observer. His patience and his attentiveness went unmatched. His perspective did too. Other qualities make the list, but I think he was thus so mostly because he didn't own anything nor had any desire to, and was always working on neglecting more. As Socrates said, *Having the fewest wants, I am nearest the gods.* If Plato was not already sitting amongst them, he was well on his way. Add to the fact that he required little to no attention and you have the recipe for someone to solve real problems in real worlds.

Even so, of all the wonderful thoughts that came from his mind, the answers he searched for remained elusive and delicate. The great qualities in man often came from the same vein as some of his worst; and by trying to segregate the two to eliminate one, you destroy the other.

~

As one could have guessed, Mary and I only intensified. Our letters were written and rapidly exchanged with each and every move of our day recorded and shared. I was able to sneak home three or four times that spring semester of 1931, telling no one except Mary of my visits, sometimes only staying a few hours and returning back to campus. We were simply untouchable to anything outside of us. The pressure in my veins was now softened and punctual. I was convinced and concluded that if only a fifth of the world had the kindness of Mary's heart and the quiet beauty it possessed, then all would know heaven as its equal by association, and hell would be a faint memory of history and civilizations that existed centuries ago.

And yet, I was mindful of what Plato referred to that day in the park. I was unwillingly aware of his notion of time and circumstance. I thought of Mary and me, and our first day of class in our first year of school, and how we sat directly across from each other. I wondered if it would have been any different if I just happened to be placed in the back of the room, or she a few rows away. I wondered if that would have mattered. I wondered how things would be between us now. I feel like I must confess here that Mary and I did not always live happily ever after. In all truth, there were times, perhaps even years that we were not very fond of each other. There were moments of roars and purrs, but more often were there days of sitting at idle. Once or twice we did everything we could to keep from stalling out. Love was always the deep and immutable bond at the bottom of it all, to be sure, but sometimes missing was its sweetness and its decoration, its cherry on top. To her core though, I blindly did love her. As to mine, I think, so did she.

But as that first winter back with Mary slowly modeled into spring, the education of me continued undeterred. I found myself seeking to be alone in the city of many. I began sensing the metronome of existence in real time. Hindsight honorably played its part and contributed to the futility, but the pendulum was accelerating at a strong and even clip; the tempo faster and faster. Whether I was at Washington Square Park staring at the weathered curves on a wooden park bench or sitting in a classroom watching my hand unconsciously manipulate a pencil with amazingly accurate and precise movements, the speed of life was palpable. My awareness of its acuity was oddly palliative.

14

The retraction of my youth reached its zenith the evening Plato showed up at my threshold wearing construction overalls and a hard hat. He carried a second and similar outfit slung over his shoulder.

"Here," he said, throwing the pair of matching overalls at me, "Get dressed. We need to get going."

"But I have an exam first thing in the morning that I just started studying for," I pathetically responded.

He had disappeared from my doorway by the time I finished my excuse, and so I obeyed his demand and found him waiting for me on the steps outside. It was a warm and windy evening in March, and from one of the opened windows of the building across the street, symphony music could be heard from a player recorder, and I noticed Plato had turned his ears towards it.

"Sounds almost perfect, doesn't it?" I said to him.

"Such sweet compulsion doth in music lie," he replied, quoting Milton in agreement, "But I wonder if we love music mostly because it's easy to love music. It requires the least amount of effort. We hate to better ourselves because it requires work and a bit of dedication, and so, we just would rather listen to music and glorify it instead."

"So," I said after thinking about it for a moment or two, "Am I lazy because I like music?

Are all things that I find beautiful are only because I'm lazy?"

"No," laughed Plato, somewhat taken aback at my appropriate rebuttal and almost matching acuity, "I agree that the most simple things are often the most beautiful, and should always be recognized and appreciated, but also, in a way, should not be dwelled upon and considered vital. Few and far between are those who think for themselves. It is a rare sport, not because of ignorance, but because of the required effort. Music, therefore, is not food for the soul, even though some insist it so."

When Plato and I spent time together, he infused such a temperate confidence in me that I was often fascinated at the behavior that resulted from it. Perhaps others he met were infected similarly, but I found it to be a quality only true friends possess: finding and encouraging things in each other that we never knew we had.

When we reached 34th and Broadway, he stopped me and said, "I want you to act like you've been coming to this place for years. Carry a look on your face like you're almost tired of being here."

With surprisingly little effort, I slipped on the hard hat that Plato had gotten from who-knows-where and walked past the construction gates and into the nearly completed Empire State Building like I was annoyed. Plato raised his eyebrows slightly and gave me a smile for my performance once we got inside, but I paid no attention to him and stayed in perfect character. As we piled into the elevator and began to move toward the heavens, Plato turned to me and whispered, "*Laputa*."

When I gave him a look of confusion, he leaned in closer to my ear and said, "There are children starving just outside on the street, unable to find food now for perhaps days, while we stand here in this small and unnecessary room that cost an extortionate fortune, which within seconds will take us to the top of the world and we will soon be able to touch the sky, unnaturally uninvited, where only birds and Gods belong."

I only stared at him and his comment, for I was by then so accustomed to seeing people living on the city streets that I hardly noticed them anymore, and so I lowered my gaze, identifying and admitting my anesthesia of reality. Instead of being elated while effortlessly flying up those 80 or so floors, I was quiet and somber, and half-heartedly wished I wasn't there, and those homeless people, if nothing else, stood in my place.

But the mind is so willingly deterred from the sadness of actuality, especially if we are not directly affected. Mine was thus so from the overpowering push of the moment and a monolithic object of iron and concrete. The Empire State Building was a monumental achievement and overtook center stage. Not only would it go on to hold the title of being the tallest building in the world for nearly 40 years, or that it solidified New York City on any world map, but also, and to some more impressively, was how quickly it was erected. It took just over 400 days from start to finish, and the night Plato and I snuck into and up it, the building was less than a month away from its grand opening.

After unloading from the elevator and ascending a few flights of stairs, and making a couple of wrong turns, we were out on the observation deck leaning over the railing, trying to decipher the microscopic cars and people on the streets.

"It's hard to tell the homeless folk from the rich ones at this height, huh?" squinted Plato, reminding me of his point of human pointlessness and my easily forgotten feelings of guilt.

We didn't hang around there long, for we knew other workers would sure to be suspicious of our authenticity, so we poked and prodded around until Plato found an external substructure of staging that ended up being completely hidden from the current focus of construction.

"What a view!" exclaimed Plato after he walked out onto the staging as if we were at sea level and simply standing on a beach, "Come look, Paul."

"Thanks, but I can see well enough from here." I said, as my body began to convulse at the thought of being out where he was standing.

I believe I inherited the fear of heights from my father, for neither one of us would climb a ladder on a bet, unless we had one foot placed firmly on the ground, and usually got one of my sisters or a neighbor to paint or repair projects any higher than what we could reach from the earth. But as the evening progressed into night, and through the heavy and thoughtful conversations Plato and I exchanged there, I slowly inched myself onto the staging further and further. With the aid of Plato's always calm composure, I was amazed to find my feet dangling over the infinite with only moderate concern. On a much different scale, it reminded me of the old maple tree near the river back home where Mary and I would climb together and sit for hours.

The strong and almost violent wind that night consistently raced up the side of the building. At times it almost lifted me off my seat, and often howled so loudly that Plato and I couldn't hear each other and had to repeat ourselves. It was so potent and sustained at intervals, that I swore I could feel the building sway, and when I mentioned it to Plato, he admitted that he noticed the same too.

We sat and talked on top of that building for most of the night without ever being bothered or distracted, just like we were on our bench in Washington Square Park. We carried on like there was nowhere else on earth we wanted to be, or possibly could be, and despite all the noise and hammering that occurred in close proximity, it felt as if no one else existed, and we were the only two that had this wonderfully esoteric birds-eye view of the world.

"I thought this would be a good time to read Squatty's letter," offered Plato as he pulled it out from his pocket.

I had completely forgotten about that letter Squatty handed to him when we said goodbye the end of last summer, and Plato observed my eyes become big and wide at the remembrance of it. He handed it to me after unfolding it.

"Read it aloud," he said, almost yelling through the wind.

I held the letter in my lap so the wind had trouble doubling it over or taking it away. I smiled at Squatty's words and perfect penmanship, and did as Plato asked me.

"*The spark you set in the sunrise has ignited my horizon; burning a liquid fuel to the caudal of my veins and back, allowing the ego and its tributaries to wave flags of white. There's a curious comfort in the burn and a truth in its casted shadow, making endings beginnings before they end, and souvenirs of you and me. Beyond anything that can show gratitude, thank you for giving me exposure to a life I never knew could exist.*"

I handed the letter back to Plato.

"I feel as though if JuJu were here," I said with a contented smirk, "he would have nothing to say to this, which would say a whole heck of a lot."

Plato laughed and then read the letter to himself, smiling thoughtfully.

"In all aspects, Paul," said Plato after folding the letter away, "In all ways possible, do you think life is more valuable now than it was a thousand years ago?"

"I guess I don't know."

"Will it be a thousand from now?"

I thought silently. There was a strange protection in the warm and hallowing wind that raced up and over us, somehow allowing my thoughts to breathe easier.

"Neither," I said, without expecting to.

"What?"

Plato tilted his head and turned an ear closer to me. I felt as though the wind was getting stronger than it was just a few moments ago, and although Plato was sitting right next to me, the air took away my words and shot them towards the stars.

"Not then and not after will anything be more valuable. There is nothing worth more than right now; this life, this instant."

Plato slowly nodded with a hint of a smile that didn't quite evolve. He then focused his attention toward the skyline saying nothing and carried a look as if he just awoke from a dream and was now reflecting upon it.

"I think we all need to find the moment," I said with growing confidence from my previous words and his reaction to them, "Time is such an impersonator of itself. It is the only thing in creation that has no other imitator and the only thing more self absorbed than those aware of it. Time plagiarizes itself, and we, like fools, allow it to do so."

I turned toward Plato and noticed a subtle yet more noticeable curve form on either side of his mouth. His cheeks almost imperceptibly drew his lips back and up.

"You know," he said without looking at me, "I'm very much glad we are friends."

It was then and there that I felt I was starting to take peeks of the world from the same angle as Plato, and although he had far better eyesight, I felt much hungrier to see, and in that regard, I subtlety altered the scenery we both admired from our vantage point.

We let the night take over and any words that desired to be exchanged were put on hold. I felt my bottom side going numb from sitting in one position too long, and when I adjusted myself, I noticed my legs were numb too, and then became scared at the somehow forgotten fact of how far up we were from the ground. A thin sweat glistened my being, and I backed slowly onto a more proximal and solid surface of the building.

Plato noticed my withdrawal, and he too, with a nod, thought it a wise move, but before he got up, he said, "The world is not so sad as it is silly, and not so silly as it is serious, and serious won't do. Alas! Forever is but a moment."

"If you had your life to do all over again," I yelled to Plato as he gathered his feet underneath him, "Would you change a thing?"

I turned my attention back into the building, carefully making room for him to exit off the staging. But when I turned back to him, he was gone. He disappeared. I looked around and couldn't see him. He vanished into thin air. No, worse. He fell. I quickly looked over the edge and saw him falling backside first, with his arms and legs stretched out, searching blindly to hold onto something that wasn't there. And then, I lost him to the night.

He must have misstepped while getting up from where he was sitting, lost his balance and fallen off the very top of the Empire State Building.

"*Plato*," I whispered.

~

There have been three instances in my life when the veil of time had been pushed aside and I caught existence at an angle where it was transparent and nonlinear; where the ghost of ourselves becomes real. One time was at my father's funeral. The last time was at Mary's side while I was holding her hand in the hospital, when she was moments away from passing, as each breath she strained was slower and more distant than the previous one. But the very first time was when I was racing down the stairs to find Plato without life. My body was entirely separate from my mind. I don't remember one step of the hundreds my body descended.

The air was frightening and odd when I finally reached the bottom of the Empire State Building; almost foreign; like I was wrapped in some sort of three-piece suit that was three sizes too small. It was as if I didn't belong in it and was suddenly allergic to the only atmosphere I ever knew. It was then that I began to sweat profusely, both from the infinite amount of stairs I had leaped down and the indisputable feeling of fear. In this very moment my body felt like it could burn down a forest with its energy. I felt like I could light the entire city of New York for years.

Looking back now I don't know which I was more afraid of, the overwhelming and unaccepting fact that I had lost my best friend, or whether the world had lost an amazing and beyond intellectual human being at just the start of his existence. I searched for Plato's body like a mad man. I knew he was no longer living but somehow thought he would still be alive, still breathing, waiting to say something wonderful and poetic to me during the last moments of life. Most of me knew that I would find him lifeless, perhaps unrecognizable, and along with the sweating and breathlessness, I began to feel nauseous at what I would discover and unconsciously slowed my search. And then, decisively, a dry and cold chill swept through me, dehumidifying my skin and fears. It started when I saw Plato sitting on a bench rubbing his ankle, slowly waving me towards him.

"Plato!" I bellowed as I ran to him on eggshells.

He didn't speak for some time, and I could only stand in front of him in a dumbfounded non-belief of all things real and imaginary.

"I'm..." he started, but couldn't finish.

The wind continued to blow as hard as it was warm, almost tropical, like those nights we spent in Brazil the summer before.

"I'm okay," he finally uttered after a moment of eternity. And then repeated himself, "I'm okay."

I guardedly sat down beside him on the bench. The construction workers shuffled in and out of the building but no one seemed to notice us and certainly no one lay witness to his landing. Plato rested his elbows on his knees, rubbing his head as if to help both of us understand. The last few minutes seemed not to have happened. The defense mechanisms of our restrained minds didn't allow us to think it so. Of all the possibilities of how Plato survived that raced through my mind during those excruciatingly silent moments, it was, in the end, the wind that had saved him. A gust, or perhaps several gusts, of perfect proportions came at the exact right angles at the exact right moments, and if it weren't for the sidewalk curb that his right foot landed half way on, he would have been injury free, as if he jumped off the bench we were sitting on. This too is what Plato concluded, almost doubting his own voice as much as his own being, and for the first time since I've known him, I had difficulty believing the words that came from his mouth. I sat muted and oddly shaped that he was still breathing, still a person, and yet couldn't imagine it any other way. My only reasoning that contained no reasoning at all was that angels had caught him at the very last moment, gently placed him on the ground and scolded him not to be so careless ever again, but this was equally as unbelievable as the first version, and my doubt of everything ever created only amplified and cured all the more further.

Plato described to me the event slowly and cautiously. He then paused mid sentence as if to catch up with his thoughts. Without any warning, my tearless and immortal hero became ephemeral and, losing all inhibition, began to cry.

"No," he answered me through his tears, suddenly addressing my question at the top of the world, just before he fell, confirming that he did not have a body double, "I wouldn't change a thing, except the chance I had to stop my sister the day she died."

Plato cried for several more moments until exhaustion set into his eyes and posture.

"How did I survive this fall," he said, turning to me, searching my face for an answer, knowing he didn't expect to find one, "And my sister didn't survive hers?"

I felt as though my heart slowed almost to a standstill with the mention of his sister. His voice cracked through his words and I was helpless to them, and could only break from his stare and look down at the ground.

"Perhaps the difference," I said delicately, "Is that you wanted to live."

"Did I?" responded Plato, almost desperately.

Plato closed his eyes and looked away. Although we were sitting side by side, we segregated emotionally from each other and turned into our own selves for private thoughts. As I gave up long ago trying to read Plato's, I was slowly getting better at reading my own. The wick of existence was now fully lit and blazing through me. My listening skills with myself were on high alert, and although my mind was always whispering to me, I never paid this much attention to it in the past. On that bench there with Plato, the whispers were loud and raw, direct and unavoidable. It transformed into its own life form, like the sea, and had secrets of its own to reveal to me and the universe. Candidly it whispered that the world seeks and demands to know answers of the trivial, while some of the biggest questions remain ignored. We sought-after the *silly*, eating ourselves up on the inside and tormenting our souls along the way. *Is there anything else we could be missing in this sphere of influence*?

I thought of Plato, and how he always reminded me that nothing has been said or done that hasn't been said or done before, but what is it that's missing? Have those in the past missed it also? Will those in the tomorrow fail to perceive it too?

And then, the whisper spoke again. It was softer and more quiet; almost inaudible. I listened closely with more focus and awareness, and kindly asked for the words to be repeated as I leaned forward on the bench to understand it at a better angle. The delayed response only intensified the moment, but alas it finally came: *Answers are but shallow echoes of insecure voices in an insufficient world.*

"Christ," Plato observed, after drying up and looking me over as I was still drenched in thought and sweat, "did you take the stairs all the way down? Why didn't you just ride one of the elevators?"

I laughed at his comical undertones as he smiled and things for a moment almost seemed normal.

"I don't know," I replied, "I guess for some reason I thought it'd be faster."

Once we got up and left that bench, we never mentioned the incident to each other again, and I, for that matter, never mentioned it to anyone until now.

Over the years I would read about one or two suicide attempts of people jumping off the Empire State Building and somehow surviving; of being blown back by a gust of wind through a window or before they even started to fall. But I never read or heard of anyone falling top to bottom and walking away from it.

The only other time I inquired about Plato's free fall off the Empire State Building was years later during my tenure as a high school principle back in New Hampshire. Our physics teacher had called in sick one day and we hadn't any stand-ins available, so I ended up substituting the substitute and watched the class myself. The day was nothing more than one long study hall, but shortly after the first bell rang I proposed an 'extra credit' question as such: "If I were six feet tall and weighed 175 pounds, and were to jump off the very top of Empire State Building, how much upward wind would be required for me to land softly on the ground without injury?"

Not knowing the answer myself, or how to go about calculating it, I was eager to read what the students came up with. Their answers ranged considerably. Some, with little effort I presumed, calculated winds up over 500 miles per hour. One was as high as 900. Most others ranged within 200-350 miles per hour.

But one student in particular, a girl named Hazel Bradford, was the last student to pass in her answer at the end of the day and caught most of my attention. She had highly detailed drawings, to scale, with keys and neatly organized equations. There were graphs and charts and even a little stick figure falling from a wonderfully drawn Empire State Building.

In the end, her answers, as she confessed, were not definitive. She stated there were too many variables to be certain. But with the perfect conditions, and precise timing and body configuration, one of the handful of answers she calculated was a sustained wind speed of only 75 miles per hour.

Her calculations inspired relief in my entire being almost instantly; not because it encouraged hope for others to be convinced of what happened, but entirely because it allowed *me* to believe. For so many years I doubted what took place and to now have hope for the probability of that event, nearly brought me to tears.

Hazel was one of the brightest students we had throughout all the years I was principle at Thayer High School. She went on to graduate as valedictorian her senior year and then, coincidentally, attended New York University. Her 'extra credit' was a homemade apple pie Mary had baked and was famous for; winning at our town's annual baking contest each and every spring.

~

It was two days before I saw Plato again. He showed up in my doorway and we stayed quiet for a few minutes, as if to give gratitude to each other and the depth and breadth of immortal moments and recent events.

"You look fully rested and recovered," I said to him.

"I'm afraid I've yet to sleep," was his condensed yet smiling response.

We stared at each other for several more moments with subtle and mutual understanding.

"I have discovered these past few days," he pondered aloud, "How many wonderful hours of the night I have wasted in a dormant state. It's an indefensible shame, really. I concede that sleep and dreams are a necessity, but the amount of thought that can be acquired and flexed and digested over the same period is unforgivable."

I made no response to him but agreed with a smile. And then, catching his demeanor and the way he leaned against the door frame of my room, I took a stab in the dark for the underlying reason of his visit.

"You're here to tell me that you are leaving this city for a very long time, aren't you, Plato," I said evenly.

"Yes," he responded.

On the train ride from Chicago back to New York City the summer before, I remembered asking

Plato about his extended family. Like his immediate one, he didn't have much to say, but did mention his grandfather he had lost just a couple of years ago. He told me that everyone hated this grandfather because he was mean to each and every person he came in contact with. He was, as Plato put it, a nasty and abusive drunk like his own father, minus the fact that he never had a drop to drink.

But as it was with almost everyone and everything, Plato was the exception. The grandfather liked him and confided in him, and they often talked for hours on end. A few weeks before his grandfathers death, he confessed to Plato the reason for being so taciturn to almost everyone he knew, especially to his own family. As it were, he had tragically lost a total of five brothers and two sisters during his childhood due to either illness or trauma, and missed them terribly because they were so sweet and kind and important to him. He in turn did not want anyone to miss him and did not want anyone to go through what he had himself, for he knew all too well how much hurt and how much damage his heart and soul sustained. He was incredibly fragile with the subject, and it proved the only time he mentioned it to Plato.

Plato remembered him a couple of years before at his sister's funeral. He sobbed uncontrollably and was inconsolable throughout the ceremony and for some time thereafter. Family members at the time could not make sense of his behavior and tried to comfort and help him, but all attempts to do so ended in them being forcefully and decidedly pushed away. They left him alone in the church until no other sobs or tears could be made, and they never learned or could even comprehend the devastation that laid waste within him of all the loved ones in his life that were lost too soon.

I could see that Plato identified with his grandfather without saying so. He seemed to adopt his belief of not wanting to say goodbye to anyone. Plato hated the idea of anything ending, because he knew all too well that everything did.

Of course I assumed there were other reasons for Plato to leave, and as much as I was against it, I was neither surprised nor even bitter when that time had come. He had more things to experience, I told myself, and in all honesty I was lucky he stayed in New York as long as he did. There was always something unexpected and light-hearted about Plato. Nothing in life was crucial to him, except life itself, and this character trait was magnificently contagious, especially and of course, with me. The last words we exchanged were not emotional, nor were they full of tears and sadness. They were instead toned with respect and happiness; thankfulness too. We spent less than a handful more times together, most of our meetings taking place at Washington Square Park.

“Plato,” I said to him as I watched him pack a suitcase on his last day in the city, “did you ever actually meet up with that girl you spoke of in Washington Square?”

"I did actually, just the other day," smiled Plato thoughtfully, "As it turned out, she wasn't as mysterious as I imagined her to be, and, equally, I think she felt the same towards me."

"I don't believe that for a second," I argued, defending my best friend.

"It's true, I'm afraid," he shrugged good heartedly, and then stood as if addressing a large audience, "She graffiti'd my heart with black ink calligraphy. Honing my weakness with her sharpened indignity!"

I laughed at his poem as he dropped to one knee with his arms stretched straight out to his sides in surrender.

"Oh verity!" he moaned, "Thou puppeteer!"

We both smiled at each other one last time.

"Plato," I said almost urgently, changing the tone instantly in the atmosphere, "please promise me you won't fade away."

Like all great things that hit you hard and leave you wanting more, I never expected to hear from him again, as strange as that may sound. In spite of how close we were at the time and the many things we had experienced together, I believed this to be an odd and eventual fact, even though he promised me that day that I would. As it turned out, Plato stayed true to his word and sent me letters almost every month for over fifty years. Although we have met up only once over all that time, there is not a day that goes by that I don't expect him to appear in my doorway carrying that smile of his. I feel confident that our friendship will one day start where it had left off.

And yet after all these years, after this flash of a spark where the only proof of time passing exists in the reflection of a mirror; or the little elm tree Mary and I planted in the front lawn that now dominates the property, I have realized that Plato is one of the most profound human beings who ever lived; that no one ever knew about, hardly even me. The world never knew of his existence. They were never exposed to his presence, never able to contemplate his views, never able to argue, futilely, to his points. Simply put, they never got the chance to learn from him. Perhaps, just a handful of us had a glimpse.

Alas, I will say this about Plato: his leaving New York City left an immense and immediate emptiness within me, and even though he did write to me over the years, it did little to pacify the reality of his absence. Indeed, I learned and harnessed so many thoughts from him, but one of the most critical and profound things he taught me was that there is no greater damage done to the mind, and even the soul too, than when you lose a true friend.

The last letter I received from Plato was almost 20 years ago. There has been no trace of him since. Not one word. I often think of what may have happened. But even though tears write these words now, I want to be clear: I do not weep for Plato, or me, or even our friendship. I weep for mankind.

~

My senior and final year snapped by faster than it took the train from New Hampshire to get to New York. Emily and I continued to camp beside each other, sitting and dancing around the flames of attraction without ever once getting burned; equally worshipping and ignoring the illusion while having fun and making the most of whatever was left in its wake. Mary and I only melted further into each other, welding our flesh and fondness of our feelings, writing letters to each other at an unmatched pace without ever once looking back.

But the sting of Plato's absence persisted. New York City was a shell of itself without him: quieter, less interesting, less alive. I knew it not without his presence and therefore it took on a different role. It was simply less of a place without him.

"Did you ever notice how Plato was so very much loaded with fun?" once observed Emily a few weeks after he left the city, "It always seemed to surround and puddle him, and at times, almost looked as if it would drown him. He was pickled and packed with a reserved yet endless energy of bursting fun, no matter how serious his words and thoughts were. It seemed to make up his entire foundation. He almost always appeared to be choking on it."

"He told me once that a sense of wonder is the secret code to life," I added, "It is an imperative for any moment. It is our only lead on immortality."

We both sat silently in agreement.

"I always thought that you and Plato would make a splendid pair, Emily," I responded with honest and warm sincerity.

"Plato is out of my league," she said directly, "It'd be like dating a god. They don't do that anymore now, at least that I know of."

~

I bumped into Copper a couple of times that final year in New York City, and one of those times we had a few drinks together, mostly reminiscing about Plato, swapping stories and even a few laughs. Yes, to my surprise, Copper was actually capable of laughing. I remembered to ask him if he knew anything about how Plato acquired those two large and heavy bags of money I helped him drag back to campus during our freshman year. He said that he did, and then told me the story.

"It's quite short and simple, really," said Copper indifferently, "He bet all that he owned on a football game. He nailed the spread perfectly. It was a game you and your team played in. Against Yale, I think it was. Yeah, Yale. He exhaustively researched both teams. He didn't want you to know about it just in case it came back to you somehow. He wanted to maintain your innocence."

"Wow," was all I said.

"What's more," added Copper, "He took all of the winnings of that money and invested it in some homeless families in the city, renting apartments for them, buying clothes and food, and, a few evenings a week, he would teach them all how to read and write. I believe most of them are still living around Washington Square Park. He kept this up for a couple of years, at least, until most of them who were old enough found work and the rest were in schools."

~

The first place I saw Emily ended up being the last place I saw her as well. We met up at Washington Square Park the day before I was to head back on the train to New Hampshire for good. With a quick hug and long frowns, and just as others who part from one another, we promised to keep in touch and never to lose our current level of devotional friendship. As she backed away from me, she curtsied a sweet and subtle bow. It reminded me of a play I went to see on Broadway that same spring where the actress ended the night in similar fashion, as the lights dimmed and the curtain fell just in front of her.

But after we turned and walked away from one another, Emily must have thought an encore was requested, for she tackled me from behind and to the ground, spinning me on my back and pinning my arms over my head. She then greeted my lips with a long and lean kiss from hers, and then, for payment, punched me square in the mouth. As I was equally angry and happy, I licked the trace of blood that formed in the corner of my smile, attempting to yell at her but was unable to form any words for nothing came out but laughs.

"Promise me now," she insisted, losing her smile and in more of a threatening demeanor than an asking one, "That if we both are not married within five years, we will wed each other, no matter the circumstance!"

"Five years?!" I laughed, "We will be ancient by then! I will need a cane at that age more than a bride!"

"Promise!"

"Okay! Okay, I promise!"

A flash of satisfaction crossed her face. Then it thoughtfully refocused.

"There are stars that listen to my thoughts," she whispered, leaning in closely to my lips as if she didn't want anyone else to hear, "Not all, but some of them contemplate my words. I listen to theirs, too. We converse by time and light. You will *always* brighten my sky, Paul McNamara. Perhaps someday I'll do likewise to yours."

As she still had me pinned to the ground, I, without thinking, went to kiss her on the mouth for the first time, which also proved to be the last. She pulled away from me just as my lips were about to make contact with hers.

"I'm sorry, I can't," she mimicked, referencing my comment to her the second time we met, "My love can do nothing more for you now. Il fait le mort!"*

And with her wonderfully thick and wavy hair that tickled my face and darkened the daylight around me, and along with the faint smell of daffodils I noticed every time we were close, she coquettishly scowled with that hint of pout she carried with her everywhere she went. Emily then punched me in the gut, stepped up and off me, and walked on her merry and determined way, with her perfect hips going one way as her uncompromising hair went the other in opposition: back and forth, back and forth; under the arch once more, and out of my life and Washington Square Park.

*"*Il fait le mort!" translation: "It plays dead!*

~

Lastly, and always firstly, was my dearest friend and my most beloved of all things. Mary and I never bothered to get engaged, unless being very much engaged toward each other counts, since the first moment we met as children in the first grade, on the first day of school, at our very first glances we exchanged with one another. I never asked her to marry me nor obtained proper and traditional permission from her father; for she and I, and everyone for that matter, knew who we were and what we were about.

We bought and settled into a house in Winchester, New Hampshire, that gently cut into the side of a hill overlooking the town. It was here that I became best friends with two of the most beautiful persons in the world. My daughters spent their childhood running and laughing up and down their steep backyard; chasing butterflies and feeding deer from their hands, filling me with a joy that only can be applied and identified by a father.

I did not tell much of this history to them for many years for I thought it mostly self-important and somnific. I did, however, take them to our old swimming hole on the Connecticut River. It was not long after Mary had passed. I had never shown them the place nor ever spoke of it before, but I told them that this was where their mother and I first said 'I love you' to each other. At the time we were both barely twelve years old.

I also told them, as I have previously mentioned, that it was the place where Mary gave me the necklace she made from her own hair, the day before I was to leave her for the first time to go to New York City, and the very same necklace I still wear around my neck. I think my daughters appreciated the place and its history, for I noticed tears on their cheeks and in their eyes as I told it. It probably didn't help much that tears covered my face too.

And in spite of my old age, I was able to clamber up a small embankment to that maple tree Mary and I used to climb together and spend most of our summer afternoons. To my subtle astonishment it was just as I remembered, as if it had not aged a day since I last stood under it, as if the wind of time had been allowed to race over and around her branches and trunk yet never through them. Standing there with memories filtering sun and shadow, a flush of wind briefly turned the leaves on their backs and I faintly heard Mary's voice singing through their softened rustle. It renewed hope to my timid memory and confirmation to my heart that it was my favorite place in the world and that Mary's voice was inarguably, in this same world, my favorite sound.

Mary was the backbone of our family, the blood of it, and the tears, the toughness, the clear headedness; the laughter. My daughters have not yet gotten over her being gone and neither have I. I don't believe any of us will. How clever Mary was in so many avenues of life, and, in her final curtain call, how endlessly clever she was to die first. How witty anyone is to do so. When I was young I wanted to live forever, like most do. But I also secretly wanted to outlive everyone and everything. This was by far the loftiest and most selfish dream I had and, unfortunately, one of the few that for the most part came true. Make no mistake, I have had a *stellar* life, but the most tragic and unspoken event in all existence is living longer than anyone you care about.

I must confess I ended up keeping two secrets from her. One of them was Emily. As Mary did not reveal those involved in her life at that time to me, so did not I to her. We kept our only intermission from each other unshared and to ourselves.

The other secret occurred first thing almost every morning after we married. I was always privately convinced that I was waking next to a princess that I did not deserve, and therefore would I often watch her in awe as she slept; with her dandelion breath that forever kept perfect and tranquil cadence, as her dormant eyelids sealed in dreams and imprisoned beauty that would only become freed with consciousness and the light of day. I was fortunate enough to be the one to usually wake first and would replay this routine over and over, mornings on end, month after month, adoring and worshipping her so. My favorite moment was the precise instant she opened her eyes for the first time, as if being born again, taking in the environment and gathering all the thoughts and pieces of who she was, all in a fraction of a second, and all in a terribly adorable and childlike manner.

Never once did I let on to this secret habit I had with her, nor ever did she apprehend me in the act. Every now and then I felt as if I was caught red-handed, but she was perhaps too sleepy to register my obsequious and abject behavior. Sometimes when I could no longer resist the temptation and when the morning air was right and light and crisp, and the little birds were happily singing outside our bedroom window, I would softly kiss her awake. Her warm and cuddly smile of recognition, sometimes involving a barely audible and short giggle, spread a joy in my being that went unequalled.

EPILOGUE

It is hard to believe the many years that have accumulated since those extended days in New York City. What a distilled trip it's been. Of all things remembered, existence itself will prove the shortest memory one will ever have. Plato believed life was an illusion. I only think time is, but perhaps they are one and the same.

Not long after Mary passed, so, too, did my quiet, sweet, and extremely funny sister, Dot. My oldest sister Irene is still living and living well; and we sometimes spend afternoons together talking of old times and such. It's funny, we still have our agitated moments as siblings, but we have never been closer than we are now, not even during the early days of our childhood.

It is true that I have given my two older siblings a bit of a hard time, even though they were always good to me and very much protective of me. As children, I remember one time distinctly when my sister Irene said that she would die for me. At the time I was too young to understand the idea of it. Perhaps I was seven or eight years of age, which would have made my sister Irene around the age of thirteen. When I asked her, in an innocent and baffled demeanor why she would do such a thing, for it seemed at the time such an inconceivable undertaking, she simply answered, "Because you're my brother."

She is now nearly 100 years old and I wonder if she ever remembers saying that to me. I will be sure to ask her soon, for soon is all any of us have. It also makes me wonder what I myself have remembered and what dreams that may have been lost along the way. In the meantime and in spite of this, I gratefully and respectively hold onto the idea of how wonderful it is to take *time for time.*

I once asked Plato if he should write a book about his life, to which he replied, "Any poor soul who ever writes an autobiography is pathetic and too self-important, for half of all of them are fabricated, most are contrived and self-promoting, and all are simply poachers of time."

So here I am, right now, writing about myself. But, if it only pleases me, I wish to end all this by sharing a bit more about Plato. When I asked him what he was thinking that day on the beach during that eternal summer of 1930, just before we departed with Squatty and JuJu on Ol' Caps cargo ship in Rio de Janeiro, he responded that he was conjuring up a new religion, but we never once got around to actually discussing it. I think though, that he consciously taught me this religion since the day I met him and every day thereafter, as I slowly and unconsciously absorbed and applied it to my own existence.

With a significant risk of failing to square his circle, and since committing heresy of the didactic here long ago, I will attempt now to translate some of his faith into words; put down a bit more of his mind, or his *motus operandi*, so to speak, as closely as I can, if at all possible, in print and on paper. Whatever I didn't hint on at the beginning of this story or throughout the bulk of it, I will endeavor to suggest here in its reluctant end. Like almost all things related to human life, I did have a few early impressions that could have related to Plato's way of observing and adjusting the self, like perhaps all of us have had, for it is *life*, and it is *human;* but for me, if ever these thoughts were sparked, they never succeeded in holding a significant or enduring flame.

There was one time as a child when I was fishing from a beaver dam of a pond not too far into the woods from our backyard. Without one nibble or any sign of fish for what seemed like hours, I lost interest from failure and decided to turn my back on the pond and follow the little stream the dam had leaked out. Not too far down had I discovered a smaller partial dam that the water flowed over quite easily, with well placed rocks wedged in amongst each other, allowing little else but water to sneak over and through. It was here between two rocks that I found not one, but three little silver fish, no longer than my index finger, aligned one atop the other, in a horizontal fashion, trapped like sardines in a can!

I had no idea how long they had been there, but astonishingly found that they were still alive; for it seemed just enough water trickled over their position to sustain them. Quickly did I go to work on trying to free the fish, but my chubby fingers were too big for this small and deep miniature canyon they resided in, and so finally a small twig I found from the riverbank did the trick.

After gently rubbing each of their bellies in a side pool where they were placed, they slowly came alive and each by turn darted off downstream as good as new. Rarely did I feel more proud then of rescuing the lives of these creatures. I was so inspired that I walked back up to the pond and directly landed four smart fish with my worm and hook and in high spirit ran the entire length home with them strung over my back. Later that evening my family listened assiduously as I retold the story to them at the dinner table, over a freshly caught dish of pickerel.

At the time I sensed the dichotomy of this small experience and the subtle urge to evolve from it, but I was unable to completely encompass the understanding. It wasn't until years had passed and upon remembering the memory had I realized human nature exists on either taking or saving. What little games it can play on itself without knowing, or resisting to know, even in a short span of a lazy summer afternoon.

As it was with this and other events, nothing seemed to stick to my ribs for the majority of my youth. As I was so spineless and mindless and easily influenced by what was so important to society or culture, or what was considered *learning* at the time, or, at any time, (for the herd is so readily corralled), these instances that I stumbled upon, that were suspiciously full of substance and meaning, and fully charged with pyrrhonic energy, fell quickly and mindlessly to the wayside. With Plato, I began to learn how to almost always land on the buttered side down; and better resist the temptation of stepping into those deep and well-worn ruts that were long ago laid out in front of me.

In Plato's religion there is no specific *corpus juris*, but if there could be one, or a general theme, it would dwell on the pursuit of anonymity. I believe Plato would, at the very least, agree to being known only and barely to himself. The need for attention is as curious as it is constant. It is a pernicious habit that we have conceded to be indispensable and now find that the only possible thing worse than not getting any is the dreadful chance of getting more than we thought we needed in the first place. Dream then, Reader, if ever tempted, of one day becoming forever unsung, for true contentment in life is freedom and true freedom is to be unknown. If you unhitch yourself in almost all ways to this learned life, if you put all your energy into the glory and recognition of being obscure; if, without any determent, you focus your efforts in the art of dedicated and beatified stalemate in this current checkmate society; if this thought in turn lights fire to the globe and proves as addictive as air, then the world will become immune to sin, war, and honor, and all the other fallible and unforgivable behaviors and concoctions of man. To be unknown is to be un-owned. In some other words, don't just swallow your pride, void it.

Plato would, I suspect, stop me here and accuse me of being too optimistic with this sphere and his faith altogether; for his religion is based on the individual only. It is *non-possessively singular*.

He would simmer my enthusiasm by simply reminding me of our *nature*; and would take further wind out of the sail by stating that it's not necessarily what is wrong with our condition that concerned him most, but rather, and much more oppressively, is the lack of interest there is to improve upon it. No one is consumed with thinking about the roots of the evil within us, let alone hacking at them. We tend to focus our energy with a few of the small twigs and perseverate accordingly. Influence is wasted through diversion and delusion. *We are too close to our work.* By damming a minute tributary we further strengthen the whole, effectually doing more harm than good. It is like trying to kill a tree by blowing the leaves off from it, when the end result is that we only strengthen its footings.

Plato would then take the final breath out of the sky by concluding that the only profitability from this faith is moral contentment and therefore stands little chance of survival. Indeed, a truth is useless if it isn't useful, but I have more hope than he, so too did Squatty, JuJu, and Mary, and if it is found to be less pandemic than imagined, at the very least he, and we, and you will be infected with this lifelong humility. Without a doubt and within a nick of time this world would be found infinitely improved if everyone didn't think so highly of their importance. Plato thought life was without question a big deal, but hardly anything of it is. Hardly anyone is ever as good of a bargain as one thinks. Hardly anyone was ever found more important than they thought they were. In the end we all simply take turns *ploughing the sea*. Discover the courage to contemplate contentment and you will find that insignificance is not only a virtue, but a necessity.

"I'm not saying that you don't matter," Plato said to me once, "I'm just saying that you don't have to."

"But if I don't matter," said I to Plato, "Who will matter to me?"

"I would like to think that you will matter more to others the less they matter to themselves, and vice versa," replied he to me.

Most of us work so hard and constant our entire lives trying to avoid insignificance. Why on earth for? I have found life much more wonderful to embody it. Certainly seek to know thyself; spend beyond an eternity to explore thyself; but well before and beyond that, ahead of any journey that begins or any anchor that is raised within; in order to have true and raw experience, seek first to *disown* thyself. Donate you to the moment you are in. Allow it to have all the attention. Push your proprietorship far and away. Don't belong to as many things in life as you can, including yourself. Be like JuJu's people and identify with what Plato observed: '*Possession is poison*.'

Ownership will always remain the root problem to the trees and branches and fruit of life. Forever own nothing. Do not give up all things in order to have everything. No, no, no: give up everything to have nothing. The word *my* is used far too often in the language of this world. Seek no reward on this because there exists none. If you must pursue, then chase after the sun and not the carrot, for there are no incentives in Plato's religion, no trophies, no acknowledgement at the end of the crumb trail. There are no mansions in heaven to reside in and own. At most, for at times it is unavoidable, be acquainted and possessive of things only by name, never by heart. Release them.

How difficult it will prove in this current society to conceive it possible or even thinkable, but it is the sole detonator to discontent. It is that secret and denied sadness we all seem to carry and covet. It leaves us wanting more. Most are overly possessive of their possessions. We forget that we have all inherited *sky front* property, but even more often do we forget to simply look up. The sky is no more valuable than the earth. Disown the world you are led to believe you own. A multitude of freedoms will instantaneously surround you.

Over the years I have commonly observed common people fighting for a position of contentment their entire lives like it was a competition. They naturally used others as a marker to judge and grade themselves; when the only report card, if ever there could be one, should forever and exclusively be found within. Sadly, any contentment is short-lived and the world spins accordingly in the wrong direction. It is no secret that we all lose perspective now and then, but our reluctance in getting it back or our resistance in continuing the infinite search for more is inexcusable. In ninety-nine moments out of 100, most people want to be somewhere else than where they are. What a waste of real time! Escape the escapes. Fixing reality is far more gratifying than running away from it. Keep your clay wet and learn how wonderful it is to be where you are, when you are. Heaven may turn out to be unnecessary.

The whispered prayers in Plato's religion, like other religions, almost always involve the insistence on never seeking acceptance and approval from others, no matter how little the abode you reside in is, or what tiny, little street you live on; in the little town of the little country of this little world, in this little universe; and the littleness that exists far and beyond all that. 'Tis a waste, a waste, a wicked waste; and will forever exist and be overplayed by your acquaintances and neighbors who desire the dry and shallow wells of recognition. Get off that bus. Walk. Collect and learn the paths of wisdom explored by others and with them find another way. Discover the soft and secret foot path to life that few know and even fewer look for. Become the church mouse in your own church of the world. Be as quiet and as poor as you've ever imagined one to be. Try not to give superfluous wealth so much charity, or blessing, or permission, for it will never return the favor if or when obtained, and will never be worth as much as a beat of a heart or one blink of an eyelid. Over-wealth gives no more satisfaction than poverty. Contented rich men have never outnumbered contented poor ones or ever will.

"The experience of witnessing a child, any child, chasing a butterfly, any butterfly, is worth more than anything ever contrived in this world since or henceforth," Plato once said to me.

A friend I met just after NYU and upon returning home, became early on in his life a self-made man of wealth. He was a classic scrooge in almost every sense, saving and pinching every penny he was ever introduced to. Starting well before his teenaged years, extremely poor though he existed, working hard and long, all days and nights, in hope for one day to retire relatively young and live the life of luxury his dreams of youth paralleled. His plan, as it was so well executed, ultimately paid off, but he discovered one small detail he overlooked when the glorious day had come to stop working. With all the money that he made over the years of his existence and all the fun things in life he confessed missing out on because of it, and how efficient and accustomed he became without all the luxuries the world had to offer, he quickly discovered that he only knew how to make money and save it; and was completely ignorant and incapable of how to spend it.

Over and over he tried to exhaust his cherished fortune but had failure far worse in multiples than he ever had in the success of making it. In the end, he had to resort back to making money because he found nothing else to offer himself or the world. He even admitted to me that the problem with redundant money was the relentless urge to make more of it. He went on to say that *quite enough* is never *quite enough* and he thought it was the very last resort to doing anything worthwhile in life. Just short of a year after his planned retirement, my rich friend with a poverty-stricken soul died unexpectedly and relatively young. He was heartbroken; surrounded by a mountain of gold that he adored like the love of his life, as so it turned out to be; of which he was ironically and most extraordinarily malignant to. He was a slave who fell madly and hopelessly in love with his slavedriver and the more he tried to love, the more the other hated.

Most men, it seems, have only one or two years of wisdom regardless of age. A person I met just recently had spoke of all the education he had, the schools and colleges he attended, the knowledge that he learned and applied to his life career. He boasted (without an ounce of prompting from me) of the houses he owned and the shiny cars he bought and collected, and how much profit he made on each and every one. Although impressive and interesting as it would surely be to some people, I soon sensed that he was telling this same story to any ear he could bend, or twist rather, for at least the last fifty years of his life, and would tell the same story another fifty if given the chance, word for word. I then found his tale to be sad and wanting; and the man telling it, with his fancy watch and his shiny shoes, to be broken and insecure. As if to add more salt to his own wound, he then proceeded to tell me how much of a busy man he continued to be and hadn't a moment longer to spare with me. It seemed as though he prided himself more on how busy he was in life than how successful he was at it. He then confessed he had less than a handful of restful moments his entire existence, and, staying true to his word, rushed himself off like he was trying to outrun daylight; when in truth he was only trying to outrun himself. To me, this was the only real thing he appeared to be genuinely triumphant at in his life.

Plato would relate this to what he called the 'only person on earth dilemma.' He questioned what any one person would actually do if they were the only one left on earth. He believed that more sooner than later, that person would live a very simplified life; an appreciated and quiet life. Nothing then would be owned. Nothing then could be bought or sold and nothing would be left to envy. Life would be a molehill. He further was convinced that if each person today could imagine themselves in this situation, if they could apply this mindset of a simple and blissful solitude within society, *any society*, each person would live a luminescently happy and anxiety free existence. Though we long for attention and praise, as we are built thus so, the pathway of life unnoticed is always sweetest, or as Plato would say more lyrically: 'Fallentis semita vitae.'

Pray each night before sleep to become as selfless as you are self-reliant. Toe that line. Pray that it becomes universally encouraged at birth and in every situation thereafter; in every city or countryside or society; and in every other kind of educational setting, including and most importantly, at home. It is the pinnacle of anything that can be learned; and although it clashes with nature, for we are born selfish, it is the only hope for mankind and the only qualifier to make the world worth saving. Make your kindness so habitual that it registers no sound and goes unremembered. Just like my own father led his own life, be selfish at being selfless.

As nonsensical as it may sound, try to avoid being discovered with whatever it is you have to offer. Be selfish on this other and only point with yourself. Politely pass on pawn promotion. Keep you close and guarded and dear; continue to polish your edges and you will find a lifetime of contented hope and the hind-sighted acknowledgement that you never needed discovering, because you found yourself.

And yet, above all, never attempt to make this religion of Plato's a law, or rule, or tradition; or ever force it on any other soul. This is a religion of one, so keep it confidential. Make it a private and personal preference. Suum cuique. Any and all crusades are strictly forbidden, so free yourself by taking little interest in the imprisonment of others. Acquire the things you believe you need, or even want, but never own them. Make that distinction. Understand the difference and abide by it. Worship a God if you wish, but possess Him not, and never allow Him or anyone else to do the same with you. You are freer than you think, freer than you can ever imagine yourself to be.

Finally, dear Reader, if you believe for one moment that I am referring to someone else, it is with hopeful regret that I am not. I am talking only and obsequiously to you. I wish to iterate one last time that there is nothing written here that is new, but for some reason it has long become unknown and forgotten. I don't mean to sound so redundant, but such is this life and so too can be the wonderful things found within it. Plato believed there's a peculiar sense in all of us that we are more contented than we know, more fitting than we feel; regardless of how hard the world tries to convince us otherwise.

And just as the day often proves coldest before dawn, so too can be the weather found in man. Souls sleep until stirred. Don't wait for the sun, but listen closely for its oncoming light. Rise in the setting frost. Prepare to give the sun's soul more hope than it ever has had before. Silently inspire it, to secretly inspire yours.

POSTSCRIPT

My name is Mary. I am the granddaughter of Paul McNamara. I often encouraged, begged, and at times, almost forced him to write this story; his story. My grandfather was a wonderfully humble and selfless man.

Our family doesn't know what happened to Plato or Emily. We couldn't find them, and we tried extensively. We believe Emily might have been an immigrant without papers; and Plato, knowing him, probably disappeared on purpose. There is no record of him anywhere after NYU besides the letters he sent to my grandfather and the few weeks they spent together nearly twenty years after their college days.

I must admit that I feel as though my grandfather's story is unfinished without knowing what happened to these two. I think my grandmother would probably feel the same way if she were still alive. Although he missed both, especially Plato, my grandfather felt differently. He thought life could never be wrapped up in a complete and tidy package. To him, it was full of loose and frayed and untethered ends and better because of it, for it directly paralleled with the mystery of it all.

At the very bottom of a large wooden box in my grandparents' attic, I found many personal things from this time in his life, including his journal. There is much in it that my grandfather did not mention in this story, and much more that I have yet to read. I hope to someday soon compile and share them with as many people as I can. This holds true with the amazing and thought-changing letters he received from Plato over the years, as they took up the better half of that same wooden box where his journal was hiding.

My grandfather passed away in the house I grew up in, where my parents still live, in the den on the southwest corner; just after sunrise on February 15, 2001. It was five days after his 93rd birthday. He is buried next to his wife, Mary, in Charlestown, New Hampshire. Their gravestones were appropriately set close to each other, and not long thereafter, they began to lean in toward one another, mirroring as they did in life. Although the stones have yet to touch, I am sure that someday they soon will.

It should not be withheld that I may have met Plato about three years after my grandfather had passed. I, too, attended NYU and have since been living in New York City. As I was waiting one morning for a train in the subway, I noticed out of the corner of my eye an older man standing beside me on the platform. It wasn't long before I felt as though he was watching me. My train arrived and as I was getting ready to file on, this same gentleman gently grabbed my coat sleeve and whispered in my ear, "You must be Paul's granddaughter."

Being a seasoned veteran of the New York City subway and the people found within it, I turned back quickly and half smiled, and then proceeded my way onto the train. It wasn't until the doors closed that I looked back for this gentleman. He was still there where I left him, watching me with a half smile of his own. Realizing all at once who he could have been, I mouthed to him the word 'Plato' and his half smile softly turned into a full one. He tipped his hat as the train slowed away and we marveled at each other until the darkness of the tunnel took over.

I take this same train almost everyday and each and every day I look for him, but have yet to find him.

Among other things, I found a few poems written by my grandfather in this same wooden box. The following was read at his funeral.

Through souls I wade
No better made
Of those that are no more
So gently laid
To be displayed
Who knows what death is for—
How much we prayed
To be dismayed
By those that we adore
In constant shade
How time makes fade
The lives we loved before.

Paul McNamara

Untitled, 7/6/97

Made in the USA
Las Vegas, NV
04 April 2021